T0288269

TO WHOM IT MAY CONCERN

Other Books by Raymond Federman

Among the Beasts (1967)
Double or Nothing (1971)
Amer Eldorado (1974)
Take It or Leave It (1976)
The Voice in the Closet (1979)
The Twofold Vibration (1982)
Smiles on Washington Square (1985)

TO WHOM IT MAY CONCERN:

A NOVEL

Raymond Federman

FICTION COLLECTIVE TWO

BOULDER • NORMAL • BROOKLYN

Published by Fiction Collective Two with assistance
from the New York State Council on the Arts. Addi-tional support
given by Illinois State University, the
Publications Center of the University of Colorado at Boulder,
Brooklyn College, and Teachers & Writers Collaborative.

Address all inquiries to: Fiction Collective Two,
℅ English Department, Illinois State University,
Normal, Illinois 61761

Federman, Raymond
        To Whom It May Concern.
I. Title

1990
ISBN: 0-932511-31-7
ISBN: 0-932511-32-5 (pbk.)

Manufactured in the United States of America

For the team: Zoe, Sticky, Patsy, Jordan,
Betsy, Robin, Jimmy, Melanie, Erica ...

[New York, Pittsburgh, Buffalo, Los Angeles]

I fear winter because it is
the season of comfort.

Arthur Rimbaud

And all we shall know of apocalypse
is not the shattering that follows but
brittleness before, the high mindlessness, the quips.

Irving Feldman

To Whom It May Concern

Listen ... suppose the story were to begin with Sarah's cousin delayed for a few hours in the middle of his journey ... stranded in the city where he and Sarah were born ... stranded at the airport ... many years after the great war which so deeply marked the cousins when they were children ... yes suppose ... it would give him time to think ... to prepare himself for the reunion in the land of promises after years of separation ... it's been thirty-five years since the two cousins last saw each other ... yes suppose ... then after the struggle with words has ended I will step back and watch the lies fall into place to shape a truth ignobly wrestled onto the surface of the paper.

Raymond Federman

That's how I see this story ... its design ... its geography. On one side, a land of misrepresentation where Sarah's cousin has been living for the past thirty-five years. On the other, far away, across the ocean, a land of false promises, a piece of desert full of mirages, where Sarah has been living her own exile for as many years. And bracketed in between, the country where the two cousins were born, and where an unforgivable enormity was committed during the war. That place will remain parenthetical. It will linger in the depth of the cousins' background. After the war they went away. He to the West and Sarah to the East.

Should this cousin be given a name? A name is so cumbersome. So limiting. It confines a being to the accident of birth, imposes a civic identity. Perhaps, for now, he can simply be referred to as Sarah's cousin. Yes, SARAH'S COUSIN. Though her name too might be deleted later on.

The cousin's plane was to arrive at 6:00 P.M. Sarah and her husband Elie have been waiting at the airport since four o'clock. This should be a joyful occasion. They should be joking at what an odd reception committee they make, wondering what he will think of them, these two zealous farm workers who for the past thirty-five years have been making things grow out of the desert sand. They should be smiling at what an incongruous delegation they are for the arrival of the famous cousin they have not seen in so many years. Instead they are troubled by a tragic incident which took place just a few hours earlier.

At noon, a bus was blown up on the main avenue in the capital city, and though the details of the bombing are still vague, everyone is talking about the attack. What a sad day for him to arrive. His first visit, and it has to be in the middle of a bloodbath. What bad luck! What will he think?

The exact number of dead and wounded hasn't been confirmed. Some say twenty-five people were killed, fifteen of them children, and more than thirty wounded. Others say at least forty people died, and many of the wounded will not survive. It was horrible. Debris of the bus and torn pieces of bodies were scattered more than a hundred feet from where the explosion occurred. Moments after the incident the police and a special squad of soldiers arrived on the scene. The avenue and all connecting streets are still closed to traffic, and pedestrians are being kept at a safe distance. Several suspects were apprehended for interrogation, and others are being sought throughout the city. As always when such incidents occur the airport is on full alert. All flights have been postponed. One can feel the tension, the anger in the waiting halls. Policemen and soldiers with guns and two-way radios are everywhere. All suitcases and bags are being searched, and some people are being pulled aside for questioning.

The cousin stranded in the middle of his journey doesn't know about the bombing, nor does anyone else outside the country. The news hasn't reached the world yet. He will learn about it later when he arrives, and he too will be saddened and dismayed, even though only a visitor, an outsider in this troubled country.

The young officer in charge of the squad investigating the bombing and questioning the suspects is called Yossi. Muscular, lanky, suntanned, arrogant in his brusque gestures and words, Yossi is Sarah's son. Of course Sarah doesn't know that her son is in charge, but she senses in her body that he may be involved. From the day he joined the Special Forces, soon after his military service, Yossi has been involved in many such terrorist attacks, arresting and questioning suspects, chasing others into remote corners of the country, engaging them in gun fights, and even killing some of them. One night Yossi was brought home with a bullet in his shoulder, home to the camp farm in the southern desert where Sarah and Elie have been living and working for as long as they

To Whom It May Concern

have been in this country. So much history to recount here. So much geography too. It was a superficial wound, but since that day Sarah has spent many sleepless nights worrying about her son, agonizing over what he does. He could be living so peacefully with them in the camp farm. But Yossi keeps insisting that someone has to do that kind of work.

While waiting at the airport, still anxious about the bombing, Sarah feels torn between happiness and despair. Happy that after so many years she will see her cousin, and desperate because she knows, she feels it, Yossi again may be risking his life. Her cousin and her son. She loves them both so much.

Yossi has never met this cousin, but he's heard a great deal about him. World traveler and renowned artist. Of course, Sarah loves Elie too, her companion of so many hard years, but she has a special kind of affection for her cousin. They shared so much during the war when they were children. So much misery and suffering. Ah so much to remember, to tell him and show him during his visit. Three weeks is such a short time.

Raymond Federman

Do you understand what I'm trying to stage here? On the one side, the cousin stranded at the airport of the city where it all started, seemingly calm and composed, and yet tormented as he reflects on his failures, anticipates with apprehension the reunion with his cousin, and remembers the wretched years during the war. On the other side, Sarah waiting for her cousin's arrival with a strange unrest in her body, her mood at once of joy and fear, concern and exhilaration. Two wanderers who years ago set out in opposite directions. He to achieve his artistic vocation, and she to help shape a sterile piece of desert into a serene and yet ruthless country.

You see what I have before me? Thirty-five years of the cousin's life in a place which, as he learned over the years, perpetuates itself on the basis of its own desultory image, and where the impact of disillusion is spent in advance. And for Sarah as many years in a land which constantly vacillates between a dream of utopia and a nightmare of destruction. And lurking in the background with its lamentable history, the country where the two cousins were born and raised, and where they managed to survived alone during the war when they were still children. How did they fall away from each other? How did they disperse? This I will tell you.

14

To Whom It May Concern

Yes, Sarah and her cousin survived, but not their parents -- his father, a younger brother of her mother -- no, they were erased. And Sarah's two brothers and her cousin's two sisters too. All of them brutally exed out ... destroyed. Their breath taken away, their bodies burned in giant furnaces. There are records of this.

X-X-X-X, that's how the cousin once drew in a letter to Sarah the design of his and her family's total absence. Their absolute erasure. She found it so disturbing that such insignificant symbols could mean so much. So poignant that her cousin should have found such a simple moving way of expressing human eradication. Maybe it's because he is an artist.

Yes, I have decided to make him a sculptor. A mad chiseler of wood, stone, and metal. In fact, the main reason for his going to Sarah's country is because the National Museum of Modern Art there is having a retrospective of his work -- a work which has brought him a world reputation of being a wild reckless and yet sensitive artist. But sculpture is often tender and violent at the same time, and Sarah's cousin is certainly a mixture of tenderness and impetuousness. His face may show kindness and generosity, but his body is in a constant turmoil of anxiety and anger. The figures in his sculptures barely emerge from the raw material. They seem either to be struggling to come out and become or else receding into a condition of non-being.

Sarah has never seen her cousin's sculptures, and often wonders if they are very modern. Cold and calculated. Rough and unfinished. Or if they are smooth figures. Sentimental and contemplative. He must be an important artist, otherwise they would not have invited him. Sarah is aware that her cousin is coming for this show at the museum, officially invited by the Ministry of Culture, but she hopes that he is also coming because he wants to see her, be with her, as much as she wants to see him and be with him, after so many years. They were so close, so dependent on one another when they found each other at the end of the war, and discovered that their parents, brothers and sisters had disappeared. Yes so close, before he decided to leave, alone, for that land of opportunities.

Sarah has often asked herself why he had to go there? Why didn't he wait and come here with her, where he belongs? They were not just cousins, when they lived together after the war, but like brother and sister. For three years they lived together in a shabby little room. Even shared the same bed. Comforted each other.

To Whom It May Concern

Though it is an inescapable fact of this story that Sarah and her cousin are survivors of the ultimate destruction, it is not its main concern. Yet it will have to be touched upon. I can already hear the objections. Not that again!

Why not? As good a topic as any and quite fashionable these days. To each his own disaster. The disaster of the street accident, the disaster of the plane crash, the disaster of racial or political assassination, the disaster of the terrorist attack, the disaster of famine, the disaster of natural cataclysm. A generalized term for calamity shared on a wide scale, causing in us a gnawing feeling of frustration. Seriously though, and this is very serious, do we have to get it again? The same old sad story? Is it a good idea to play the same melodrama as before? The same old tune? Hey buddy, aren't you tired of playing the same song over and over again? No doubt it is a powerful theme, the reconstruction of a traumatic past. He thinks he can make a great book out of it so long as he does not repeat himself too much. But he worries, have we not had enough of that unforgivable enormity? And yet, it will have to be touched upon. How the two cousins managed to survive during the invasion, and how they wandered far away from each other to be reunited years later. That's the story I want to tell.

17

The question before me, however, is not of the story. The story? Always the same. The question is of the tone and of the shape of the story ... its geometry. Yes, how to stage the story of Sarah and her cousin?

How to begin in order to recount the essential without tumbling into sentimentality, and yet with just the right emotional impact? I keep searching for a possible beginning, a ready-made model. The kind of opening that sets everything in place and makes the rest of the story happen by itself. I find some, try them, rephrase them to serve my purpose, just to see if they will launch the thing. Throw them away.

The other day I toyed with this one:

Sarah was bathing her doll in the kitchen sink when the wind of her misfortunes began to blow. The plaster walls of the shabby room lost in the noise of the great war trembled down to its foundation with the first attack.

I dismissed it. Too lyrical for me. Too melodramatic. I even tried the good old Once Upon A Time, but even that doesn't work anymore.

To Whom It May Concern

We're not talking about a fairy tale here, we're talking about a story which in the process of being told might become the absolute truth.

How to begin then? Perhaps with a detour, a delay at the center of the story. This way: imagine a man in his early fifties, thick short grayish hair (you know, combed forward Roman style), sort of handsome, stocky but not fat, in great shape for his age, loves to play a mean game of tennis, and golf too (and yes, yes of course, loves a good fuck), a face marked by a mixture of determination and maliciousness, kindness and cunning, hard to tell at first glance if he is an intellectual or a businessman. He himself often marvels that so much incongruity has been assembled so awkwardly into a single being. A bit of a prominent nose.

The fact of starting this story by focusing on this man can be justified by saying that he entered the world under the sign of Saturn, the planet of detours and delays. As we encounter him, by chance, this man is going from one part of the world to another. A long journey, from here to elsewhere. His first visit ever to that distant country, and a difficult decision for him to have made. That's important.

19

Raymond Federman

It's April 30th, many years after the war. The Great War, central to this story since it affected its characters so dramatically ... and traumatically. April 30th, because this journey must coincide with the exact date when the dictator who started that great ugly war shot himself in some underground hideout when his armies were defeated.

Upon landing for a scheduled stop across the ocean the man's plane is delayed by two hours. That two-hour delay will be crucial to the story, to the shape of the story. Everything will be contained in that delay.

A minor mechanical problem, the passengers are told as they are asked to deplane and proceed to the waiting lounge. Coffee and croissants will be served. Nice local touch. Some of the passengers wonder if it is really a mechanical problem or something more serious. A bomb threat perhaps. After all the plane is going to a country constantly threatened by acts of terrorism. Everything connected with it these days is dangerous and problematic, including this story. Yes it will be a dangerous undertaking, risking the absurdity that lies in wait for excessive emotion.

The man appears calm, aloof. He has settled into a comfortable seat in a corner of the waiting lounge to read, but is unable to concentrate on his book. His thoughts are like waves breaking on a rock. He cannot pursue them as they splatter and dissipate before him. Here he is in the place of his birth where years ago so much happened. He turns the same thoughts over and over in his mind as he contemplates a cynical smile.

During the second year of the invasion, on July 16 -- to make it more authentic -- the bleak day of the great round-up, when their parents, brothers and sisters, and more than 20,000 others who had been declared stateless by the government were arrested, Sarah was nine and her cousin twelve. Since they lived in different sections of the city, neither knew that the other had escaped the round-up, and that that day they were thrown into the vast incoherent group of potential survivors. For the next three years, Sarah and her cousin wandered separately until they found each other at the end of the war. Both were deeply marked by what they experienced, and even today their survival does not make sense to them, even though they are reconciled to the excess of life they were given by fate.

Beginning at four in the morning, on that July 16, those repulsive people (as they were called by the government) were seized in the city. Arrests were made by the occupying troops and the collaborating militia. In two days, 21,884 of them were captured, including 9051 children. Men without families were trucked directly to the train stations for immediate dispatching. Parents and women with children were taken to a huge indoor arena. A highly placed bureaucrat in the government imagined that the herding of thousands of children and adults into the dismal spaces of that stadium would recreate for that vermin, as he called them, the familiar ordeal of their mythical past. For four days the prisoners were penned up without food. A single street hydrant supplied the water, and a dozen portable latrines were the only lavatory facilities. Several women gave birth during those four days without medical attention. Forty-six people died, sixteen by suicide, and a number went mad. A triple epidemic of measles, scarlet fever, and diphtheria broke out. Many women were sexually abused by the guards, and three little girls were found gagged and unconscious beneath the seats of the stadium, their thighs smeared with blood. On the fourth day, the children were separated from their parents. The adults were dispatched in one direction, the children in another.

This Sarah recently read in a book entitled TO WHOM IT MAY CONCERN. Even after all these years, like her cousin, she seems to have a need to verify the details of that moment in history which changed the course of her life. She often tries to imagine how it must have been in that place where her parents and brothers were taken.

22

To Whom It May Concern

What did they do there? Did the soldiers hurt them? Were they hungry all the time? Did they see each other? Were they allowed to speak to each other? When they died did they die quickly, or did they suffer for a long time? Did they watch each other die? Were their bodies remade into objects or were they thrown into that big hole with all the other twisted human carcasses shown after the war in photographs and newsreels?

Sarah often sees herself as a little girl standing naked in a torture chamber watching her two brothers being mutilated. She wants to reach for them to save them, but she is ashamed of her nakedness, and while with one hand she covers her eyes with the other she hides her sex. In this scene her brothers remain the chubby little boys she last saw, on that morning of July 16. She has never been able to imagine them as grown men, though over the years she has often fantasized, and even made herself believe that a man, a tall handsome man she does not recognize at first, appears on her doorstep and says to her: I am your brother, I survived, I have been looking for you all these years, I searched in every corner of the world for you. Yes, it is her brother Benjamin, now she can tell because of his eyes, his pale gray eyes soft and transparent, just like hers.

Raymond Federman

It is always Benjamin, the younger of her two brothers, who survives in her fantasy, never Simon, the eldest, who was too weak and too sickly when he was a child to have had a chance. Sarah knows that those whose parents, brothers or sisters were destroyed during the war often dream, daydream that one of them escaped and has been wandering the world in search of family survivors, but she is troubled that it is never her father or her mother or her older brother who survives. It is always Benjamin, little Benjamin with his pale gray eyes and his rosy cheeks. She wonders if her cousin also resurrects his parents or his sisters this way? She will ask him. Perhaps his little sister. She was the same age as Sarah. They often played together. Jacqueline was her name. She was so beautiful with her long curly hair and her big black eyes. She wanted to be a ballerina.

Why always Benjamin and not the others? Perhaps because Sarah's son looks so much like him. Sometimes when she is alone, Sarah takes out the only photograph she has of her brothers and studies it. Though she can barely make out their faces in that faded brownish picture, she tries to find family resemblance with her own two children. Often she cries quietly while looking at the little boys in short pants with their neatly combed hair. She cries not because she feels sorry for herself (in this land of rock and sand she has learned to suppress self-pity), but because it's good sometime to cry. That's what she tells Yossi who

24

To Whom It May Concern

scolds her whenever he finds her sitting alone in front of that photograph, her eyes wet with tears. You and your history, he tells her. Don't you think it's time to forget? Mother, you've been in this country thirty-five years, it's this life now, this place which you helped build with your own hands that matters, and not those wretched memories.

Ah Yossi, so strong, so tough, so committed to this land where he was born. He understands so much, and yet so little. How can she explain to him that perhaps without that sordid history there would not be a country for him? What cringing irony! How can she explain to her twenty-five year old son who has already fought two wars and killed dozens of human beings that these two little boys in short pants frozen in that photograph are his uncles. Uncles are supposed to be men breathing of worldliness and generosity -- men with bushy mustaches and broad shoulders who smoke pipes, always bring expensive gifts, and tell marvelous stories of their travels in the world. Uncle Benjamin, Uncle Simon, oh how Sarah wishes she could have heard her children speak these names. Uncle Benjamin, tell us of the time when you were hunting in the jungle and almost got devoured by a lion! Oh Uncle Simon, tell us again how it was when you were a sailor and your ship sank in the ocean? Yes that's the kinds of stories uncles are supposed to tell their nephews. Stories full of exaggerations and lies, stories that make little boys and girls dream of adventures in faraway places. Uncles are not supposed to be remembered as dead children.

Sarah often wonders if Benjamin would have been like Yossi. Yossi she loves him so much. Her brother-son. How is it possible for these family lines to get so blurred? Can a son ever become a brother to his mother, or is that against nature? How is it possible, she often asks herself, that she is here, in this beautiful place, still alive and almost satisfied with her existence, and not her brothers? Who made that decision?

When the soldiers came, on that morning of July 16, little Sarah was not home. Her mother had sent her to the bakery, just around the corner from where they lived, to buy a loaf of bread. The bakery was unusually busy that morning, the streets too, even though it was still early, not even seven o'clock. Several women were gathered at the counter talking in hushed voices, and it took Sarah a while to squeeze past them to pay for the bread. She was holding the money and the ration coupons tightly in her hand, feeling very grown-up among these women. Sarah loved to go to the bakery because the baker's wife, a very fat but very nice lady, would sometimes give her a piece of pastry, just like that, for free, as a gift, even though everything was rationed then.

To Whom It May Concern

Sarah was the favorite of all the shopkeepers in the neighborhood. The Little Mouse, they called her. She was so shy. Always holding her mother's hand or skirt. She was often told how pretty she looked with her curly brown hair and her pale gray eyes. And so well- behaved, so polite too, the people in the neighborhood would say to her mother. But a bit fragile, you know. Much much too skinny for her age. Yes, of course, it's difficult these days with food and everything else being so scarce, but you should try to give her more to eat.

Sarah liked the chocolate éclairs best. Now don't tell your friends in school I'm giving you this, the woman at the bakery would whisper to the little girl, frowning and shaking her index finger at her, or else you'll get no more cakes. It made Sarah feel important to go buy the bread alone, without her brothers looking after her. Usually the baker's wife made Sarah eat the pastry right then and there in the shop, but if the place was busy and no one was watching, Sarah would take the éclair home and share it with Simon and Benjamin. She would carry it cupped in the palm of her hand, as if it were a wounded bird, trying not to crush it, though the chocolate on top of the éclair would slowly melt between her fingers, especially in the summer, when it was hot.

On the morning of July 16, no one at the bakery seemed to notice her. The baker's wife gave her a loaf of bread but no pastry. When she arrived home, she found the next door neighbor standing on the landing in her bathrobe. The woman told Sarah that her parents and brothers had left with the soldiers.

Sarah did not comprehend what the woman was saying, nor the immense consequences of what had happened. She just burst into tears, and rubbing her wet eyes with her little fist, she stammered, why ... why didn't ... why didn't they wait for me? Why didn't they ... wait?

Her mother did not leave her behind by chance. Perhaps out a dark premonition, she sent Sarah to buy bread deliberately. This Sarah came to understand after many years of replaying the moment in her mind. But why her and not her brothers? Or at least one of her brothers? Why not Benjamin? Did her mother believe that someone in the neighborhood would take pity on her little girl and save her? What instinct dictated that gesture?

Sarah often wonders if faced with a similar decision of having to save only one of her children, her son or her daughter, which of the two would she choose? She knows it would be Yossi. Yes, she would not hesitate, Yossi would have to survive, and she feels no guilt about that, for she knows that even today, as in ancient times, a mother may have to make such a sacrifice.

The neighbor, whose husband had already left for work, took Sarah into her apartment and tried to console her. She gave her a bowl of warm sweet milk, told her to stop crying, that there must be some mistake, that everything would be fine. You just wait here with me and you'll see, your parents and brothers will come back soon. I'm sure the soldiers are only checking their papers. It's because your parents ... you see ... they are foreigners. It's a routine matter. They always have to check foreigners. Really I don't see any other reason for the soldiers to take them. But by mid-morning the woman realized that she could be in trouble if she kept this little girl. Recently the government had issued strict ordinances about hiding stateless people or helping them escape. And besides, her husband, who often made remarks about these dirty people, these foreigners who come to our country to eat our bread, would be furious at her for doing such a stupid thing.

Trying not to show her nervousness, the woman told Sarah that since she was separated from her parents, because her mother had sent her to the bakery just when the soldiers came, the best thing to do was to

Raymond Federman

go to the militia's headquarters and explain the situation. I'll take you there myself and tell them what happened, the neighbor told Sarah while hurriedly getting dressed. We'll tell them how your mother sent you to buy bread just before they came. They'll understand. We'll tell them it was a mistake, they'll find your parents and put you with them. I don't see any other way.

Though Sarah hardly knew this woman (her parents never talked to these neighbors who lived on the same floor), she was quickly convinced that it was the best thing to do, but she was concerned about the loaf of bread. She didn't know if she should take it with her to the police station or leave it with the woman. Her mother would be angry with her for being careless with bread.

Leave the bread here, the woman told her, I'll keep it for you, and you can get it later when you come home with your family ...

Well, enough for now. I know I've been negligent in our correspondence. The past few months have been hell. I was hiding in the basement of my own despair, perhaps even enjoying being there. A lovely lonely season in hell. One night, in the filthy darkness of that hole, the entire hope of humanity vanished from my mind. It felt good.

To Whom It May Concern

It felt like the end, like the final resolution. But now I have emerged ... resurfaced. Once again I must confront that avalanche of simultaneous events we call life.

Yesterday I stuck my nose out of the window. Winter is here. The trees and the indecisive birds in the trees told me so. It's cold, windy out there, unfriendly. I fear winter because it is the season of comfort, as Rimbaud once put it.

This morning I spoke a few words to Sam. When you visited here last he had fleas and together we gave the little guy a mean scrubbing in the bathtub. Remember? What a mess. Oh by the way, Didi the cat was ... had to be put away. Sixteen years old and still arrogant, especially with his buddy Sam, Sam-the-Timid as we call him. Didi had developed a cancerous growth in his throat. Couldn't eat anymore. His skin was coming off his bones, and his hair falling off his skin. We watched him day after day become an ugly ghostcat right before our eyes. We got this amazing letter from the vet.

Please accept the sympathy & condolence of the entire staff of Sheridan Animal Hospital -- the letter said. The loss of a pet that has been ill or injured carries an emotional toll that only people who care

31

deeply for animals can appreciate. You can rest assured -- the letter went on -- that the ominous responsibility of euthanasia is not taken lightly by us. We weigh the physical status of the patient, the disease processes & the chances of recovery. Based on these factors it is sometimes more humane to elect euthanasia. We hope that we have helped you through this most difficult of times in the life of a pet owner. If we can be of any further assistance please do not hesitate to contact us.

What a touching piece of writing. Those vets have style. We didn't know if we were supposed to laugh or cry, go into mourning and wear black for a year. Imagine: If we can be of any further assistance ... How about trying some of that painless death on me? That might solve a lot of things.

Yes, I spoke to Sam, and I think he understood what I was saying. He must have been wondering where I had been all this time, and I suppose also where Didi disappeared to. He wagged his tail happily and rushed stupidly to the door whining for a walk. Around here we never say the word, we spell it out -- W.A.L.K. The little guy goes crazy whenever he hears the word, even if we say it in French or in German. It's been months since I double- u-a-l-ked Sam around the block and watched

To Whom It May Concern

him piss on every tree trunk in the neighborhood. Yes, he must have been wondering about my absence.

You ask if I am writing. Haven't been. More than a year now. Not a thing. Not a damn thing. Total irresponsibility toward my work. I used to be able to weave myself into imaginary stories of accomplishment, but not lately. Once in a while I look at my old books in the study, those I scribbled these past twenty-five years. I touch them, turn them over in my hands, and then curse them. Useless books out of style, probably out of print. They feel like abandoned objects.

The other day my daughter on the phone (collect of course) from the big city said to me, oh without malice, lovingly in fact: Hey Pop, I think I know what your epitaph will be, I mean, you know, what should be written on your tombstone -- OUT OF PRINT!

What gentle brutality. That kid always finds the right words to fragment her old man's face into a smile. How we miss her. Since she left there is a hole, a huge emptiness in the house. Her loud music has stopped, her little noises, her unpredictable words. Oh how we miss her giddiness, her gloom, her gestures of anger, her moments of fear,

33

Raymond Federman

her mimicry of adult frustration, her impatience, her little floods of helplessness in the face of some easy problem.

She's got it right though, there is brutality in what we're doing? For more than a year, since I finished the last book, I was vegetating in the immense space of my days, not to mention the horrible holes of my sleepless nights. The time of my days always seemed too short for it to be worthwhile starting anything, and yet too long not to try to begin anyway. So I would begin something, and begin over and over again, the same something, but time ran out before I could keep it going, before I could bring together the pieces I had scattered over the day. And the same, same again the next day and the day after. I felt stranded in this elasticity of time with my stalled words in distress. And so, my head full of doubt, my body in panic, I did nothing, nothing but contemplate my own lethargy and the futile gestures of my non-writing.

But now things seem to be moving again. What do you think of what I told you of Sarah & her Cousin? Is there a book here? We addicted word-idiots cannot withdraw into ourselves too long, for we would then have to give up writing, and that would be total darkness. That is why I came up from my basement of despair to ask for your companionship

34

in this new adventure. Write soon again. I need words from you. Also tell me about you, the wife, the kids, the pets. About the birds in your trees. Your book, your winter-book, if there is one going -- on-going. More soon then.

To Whom It May Concern

Sunday, November 28

What a good reply. What you say gives me courage. So you think there are possibilities here. The book of Sarah & her Cousin? A book for us to do or undo together. A joint enterprise. And why not. Then I will lean on you. Use you. Abuse your patience and friendship. A friend, André Gide once said, is someone with whom one does a bad deed -- un mauvais coup.

What a story I have on my hands, you say. Paint it richly, thickly. Shellac the damn thing with layers of reality. Get copies of LIFE MAGAZINE of that period and look at the faces there and get those faces inside you.

Raymond Federman

What a great idea! Fictitious life created from real LIFE MAGAZINE pictures. I could even stick some of the pictures inside the book and have a technicolor story full of solid historical facts. But listen, historical facts are not important, you know that. Besides, they always fade into banality. What matters is the account and not the reality of events. So once again I am contemplating a story which will be nothing more than the speculations on ways to tell that story. I am incurable. Perhaps this time while delighting in form I'll manage to tell a real story. Remember how Blake put it: Fire delights in its form.

The other night, three in the morning, out of a half-sleep, as if continuing a dialogue we started during the day, my wife says to me: the problem with you it's always form, form, always form! And me turning to her in the dark: yes but you see, form gives me balance, it makes me happy. Unable to fall asleep we turned on the television and watched a porno flick.

It's been a good week. It ended cheerfully, although I got there by way of an abyss of anxiety. No I have not started to write, I'm not ready. Might be weeks, months before I can commit myself to paper. I have to visualize the whole thing, hear the voices, draw the geometry before

To Whom It May Concern

I can get going. I set dates of departure for myself, but I keep postponing them.

Sarah and her cousin need to be situated in the proper frame -- a place of perfect certainty where something fundamental can be said about them. But you raise a good question about Sarah's cousin. Why am I reluctant to give him a name? I don't know. I've been toying with possible names for him, all of them utterly inappropriate and therefore immediately dismissed. He may be too close to me to foist a false name on him. Perhaps eventually the necessity of a name will become apparent. But for now I feel he should remain a distant unnamed listener of Sarah's story, even though his story overlaps hers.

Then you ask why am I so hazy with time? Why don't I give the exact dates when all this happened? And where too? Is it some kind of secret?

What difference does it make when and where it happened, since none of it is verifiable. We're not dealing with credibility here, but with the truth. That's not the same. Certain truths do not need the specificity of time and place to be asserted. A war is a war, doesn't matter where and when it happened. And suffering is timeless. We all suffer a form of exile the moment we are born, what difference does it make when or where it begins.

Since this story is still in the speculative stage, even if I were to give exact dates, these would have to be manipulated as the story progresses. That's inevitable. Dates give history a semblance of stability and continuity. In this story there cannot be stability and continuity.

The only stable fact is that exactly thirty-five years ago the two cousins were separated and went in different directions. He was eighteen then and Sarah fifteen. What they are now seeking in this reunion is the meaning of that separation -- the meaning of their absence from each other. Therefore, instead of questioning the when and where of their story, you should ask how absence has marked their lives and shaped their personalities. Yes, what should be questioned is the composition of that sculptor I have parked like a statue at one airport, and that of Sarah waiting for him at another.

The sensibility that is skeptical and ironic in him, especially about his own misfortunes and failures, the temperament that is emotionally charged and high-pitched and accepts itself as such without seeking refuge in calmer realms, the imagination that is humorous and outrageous in him and yet serious and gloomy at the same time that it perceives itself in one great quality, the ambivalence of opposites, these I will carve into his character. Though he has lived many years in the same country, he has remained an obstinate foreigner in his manner of speaking and acting, and yet not a solipsist as one would expect from such an existence. Quite the contrary, an incurable optimist, though lately he too, like me, has been residing in the cellar of his own despair.

As for Sarah, this is how I imagine her: a sensitive middle-aged woman, still quite attractive with her great crop of hair, her fair skin and pale gray eyes. She too is caught in this ambivalence of opposites: shy but tough-minded, idealistic and yet down-to-earth, sentimental and yet unflinching in her emotions.

Sitting at the airport, the book still on his lap but not reading now, the cousin is thinking about Sarah. Though the two of them have sent each other photographs over the years, he can only remember her as the young woman she was, thirty-five years ago, when he left her on the platform of the train station.

Raymond Federman

He had already put his suitcase on the train and placed his jacket on a seat to reserve it, and had come down on the platform to give Sarah one last hug before the departure of the train which was to take him to the boat. What a miserable boat! And what a terrible crossing it had been! He smiles as he remembers the boat and how confused he must have looked, but then his thoughts return to Sarah and he sees her standing on the crowded platform -- skinny fifteen year old woman-child desperately trying to hold back the tears in her pale gray eyes as the two of them embraced one last time before the train started rolling.

Unconsciously he whispers what he used to call her then -- Little Bug. Skinny and furtive like a frightened insect, she was always huddling in corners of rooms, against walls, as if she wanted to disappear or hide inside these walls. It took many years for Sarah to recognize and accept the fact that her death was behind her, and that she could walk and breathe outside of fear. He loved her so much, tried so hard to care for her after they found each other at the end of the war. For three years the two cousins lived together in a room they had arranged in the basement of a building demolished by bombardments. They slept in the same bed, a mattress thrown on the floor. He was everything to her, a brother, a father. And a mother too. Yet, when the day came for him to leave, he abandoned her. He had to go. A vague necessity

42

To Whom It May Concern

was pulling him away. Something unresolved inside him. Unresolved in his hands. It was not an easy decision. The whole matter of the visa happened so quickly and so unexpectedly.

It'll only be for a few months, he kept repeating still holding her in his arms, on the platform of the train station. You'll see, once I'm there I'll find a way to bring you. I'll send money. I'll send you a ticket for the boat. I'll go and talk to the people at the emigration office and I'll tell them I'm your only family. They'll understand. I'll explain everything.

Originally the two cousins planned to leave together, especially after they found out that their parents would never return. Over there maybe things would be better, they would start a new life and forget ... but Sarah was denied a visa because she failed the medical examination. The doctor at the consulate found a spot on her right lung. Oh nothing to worry about, the doctor said, it's not serious yet, nothing that cannot be cured with good nutrition, lots of fresh air, and of course the right treatment. She'll be fine in a few months. However, the good doctor was sorry, but he could not approve her visa. It's against the emigration law to grant visas to people who are not hundred percent

43

healthy. For weeks and months, Sarah and her cousin agonized over what to do.

l won't go alone, he kept saying, though he knew all along he would go. I'm not going without you. No, I won't leave you behind. I don't want us to be separated any more. But Sarah kept arguing, as if already the tough-minded woman she was to become, that it would be silly for him to give up his visa now that it had been approved after so many months of waiting and hoping. He let her convince him, and finally they decided that he would go alone, and that when she was cured -- in a few months, isn't it what the doctor said? -- she would join him. Yes, that's the best way because by then you'll be settled and it'll be easier for me to come. Don't worry, I'll manage by myself. I'm not a child anymore, she said straining to hold back the tears.

That was thirty-five years ago. Eventually Sarah also left with a group of young people who like her had lost their families in the war. But she went to a different place. She went East, to a country full of promises. It was, perhaps, the dry desert air of that place which erased the spot on her lung.

To Whom It May Concern

The scene on the platform of the train station fades as the cousin drifts further back in time to the day he and Sarah found each other at the end of the war, when the country was liberated. It was in May. He saw her wandering in the old neighborhood, just like that, not far from where she used to live before it all happened. She was roaming the streets, as he had been doing himself for the past three weeks, since he came back to the city from the south, searching for relatives who may have survived and also returned from their hiding places. Lots of people were doing that then all over the city, especially in Sarah's old neighborhood which was suddenly regaining life. It was as if the whole city had turned into a giant game of hide-and-seek. You can come out now, the war is over!

He had left the farm in the south where he was working for the past three years, convinced that when he reached the city his parents and sisters would already be there waiting for him ...

The farm! I'll have to tell about that too. I mean, how still a boy he worked hard, like a beast of burden, during the three years he spent on that farm hiding from the soldiers, and how lonely and homesick he was, and how his body hurt all the time from the brutal work -- his hands especially, always full of sores, blisters and cuts. He was a clumsy city boy, twelve years old, but growing fast in his body beyond his age. He had no sense then of who he was and who he would become. For the moment he was just a farmer, not by choice, but a farmer anyway. The crude and vulgar mode of existence of the people and animals on the farm had taken over his whole being, even though he did not comprehend the indifferent violence of reproduction and death which surrounded him. He felt dirty all the time. Prisoner of that dirtiness. Oblivious to himself and the sordid affairs of the world, he could not imagine anything about himself in the future. All his thoughts, dreams, fantasies were about the past -- the vague and confused past. Day after day, from early morning to late evening, he toiled in the fields absent from himself. From the day his parents and sisters were arrested, on that July day, and he escaped by chance, wandering in the countryside until he was taken in by these farmers who needed help, he felt a strange dissociation from himself, as if suddenly cut off from the natural expectations of life's possibilities. His existence stalled, he was resigned to a condition of temporariness and fell into a state of obscure confusion. Such feelings were in glaring contrast to the self-confidence and recklessness of his father, who was an artist, a painter, and who always tried to instill in his son the same confidence, same drive and recklessness, even though aware that everything always results in failure. The boy had great admiration for his father, a wild unpredictable man who held a whole world of beauty and delight at his fingertips before his life was brutally interrupted at the age of thirty-five. On the farm, the boy was miserable with his own being. Some intolerable discontent was at work in his body, and it centered upon the most immediate physical organ of contact with the world, his hands, his fingers. The same hands and fingers that would later make of him an artist like his father. Their physical appearance upset him. His hands were always dirty and rough and sore and red, and he could never get his fingernails clean ... But I am digressing here.

He had returned from the farm in the south all the way to the city on top of a tank. A tank of the victorious armies which liberated the country. What a happy journey. He was going home. His mother, his father, his sisters, the whole family would be there waiting. He was certain of that. Like so many he survived with this false hope, and now he was racing toward that delusion.

He stood on the tank and for hundreds of miles he sang songs with the soldiers. It was beautiful! He was the mascot of the tank crew. Mobs of people along the roads, in the villages and all the country towns were waving flags and singing the national anthem -- Children of the nation rise and walk into the days of glory and together let us destroy tyranny! The soldiers were kissing all the girls and throwing candies and cigaret-

Raymond Federman

tes to the people. Just like in the movies, the bad movies made of all this later on. He didn't care, he was going home.

As he wandered in the old neighborhood, he saw her, his little cousin Sarah, across the street, standing on the sidewalk, as if waiting for someone, as if returning for an appointment made years ago, but with a look of anguish on her face because the person had not shown up. They recognized each other, even though they had both changed a great deal. Older by three years, but also marked in their bodies, in their faces, by what they had endured. There was sadness in their eyes, and their gestures were slow and tired. She stood there, frail and disoriented, as if she had just risen from a hole in the ground. She was twelve now, but already a woman in her body. After a moment of hesitation, they rushed toward each other and embraced, right there in the street, held one another tight for a long time. It's you, it's you, they kept repeating while wiping the tears from each other's faces ... it's you!

As the cousin sits in the waiting lounge of the airport, sipping hot coffee from a styrofoam cup, he sees himself standing in the street, holding little Sarah in his arms, and hears like a distant whisper the hoarseness in her voice as she cries out, it's you, it's you! Again he tries, as he has

48

tried so often over the years, to recount to himself the story of Sarah's survival. But he's not sure if he is remembering what Sarah told him or if he is inventing a story for her, mixing his own survival, his own story with hers, his own words with hers.

When they were living together after the war, they often tried to tell each other what happened after their parents were taken away, but they could never get to the end of their story, they could never bring it out of themselves. At night, lying close to each other on the mattress, they would try to make the other tell the story, but after a while it would stop, disintegrate, dissipate into incomprehension as if it refused to be spoken. Sarah's heaving chest and the quiet tears rolling slowly down from her eyes would stop the words. Her cousin would take her in his arms to comfort her -- it's alright, it's alright, you don't have to go on. What matters is that we are here together ...

This is what I started telling you. Remember? I was describing how the woman next door told Sarah to leave the loaf of bread with her, and how she was going to take her to the police station so she could be put with her parents. Well, let me go on, just as Sarah's cousin is trying to do as he waits for his plane to take off. Listen ...

Before taking Sarah to the police, the neighbor combed and braided her hair and straightened her dress. (The woman's fingers hesitated as they touched the patch, the yellow patch sewn on the dress). She pulled Sarah's socks up and fastened the loose buckles of her sandals. Told her how pretty she looked. She even asked Sarah if she needed to use the toilet, because, you know, once we get to where we're going it may not be easy for you to go. Sarah said she didn't have to now. Then holding the little girl's hand, as a mother would that of her own child, the woman led Sarah down the stairs and out into the street. It was hot that day. The sky clear, distant and uncomplicated. A lovely July morning.

Freedom Day, the most important national holiday, had been observed only a couple of days earlier, and decorations were still hanging from the lamp posts. Though the celebration had been somber and subdued but not prohibited (the only thing forbidden during the occupation was singing the national anthem), a little tremor of hope for freedom and the good life of the good old days had circulated in the streets of the city on that day. But now everything was back to the drab normality of the moment, except the weather, but then the weather is always indifferent to the abject affairs of mankind.

To Whom It May Concern

With a firm grasp on Sarah's hand, the woman walked briskly toward the militia's headquarters, a ten minute walk. To get there they had to cross The Royal Square.

In the old days, before the people overthrew monarchy to set up the Republic, the kings and queens used to parade on the Royal Square in their fancy carriages. Yes, that's what they celebrate on Freedom Day -- the beginning of The Republic. Ah, The Royal Square! So grandiose. One of the most beautiful spots in the world. Dates back to the 17th century. But the day when Sarah was being led by the hand toward the unimaginable condition of non-being, army trucks lined the entire perimeter of that historic square with its arcades, its red cobblestones, and its rows of trees symmetrically trimmed (chestnut trees, I think, but I'm not sure), and where a plaque on one of the buildings indicates where the most celebrated national poet once lived. Sarah and her brothers had often stood in awe in front of that building when they crossed the square on their way to school. They couldn't believe that the country's most famous poet had lived right here so close to their house, up on the third floor, behind those windows? Sarah knew by heart several of his poems, and once she had to stand in front of the whole class, on that special day when the nation celebrates its dead heroes, to recite one of the poet's patriotic odes because she was the only one who knew all the stanzas. It was called Ode to the Dead. Even today she remembers fragments of that poem, and sometimes while doing her work in the desert she recites them to herself. She smiles when she catches herself mumbling those insipid words.

Do you know that poem? It's really something. Here, I'll give you the first stanza in a rough translation:

> Those who piously died for the country deserve
> That the people come and pray at their coffins.
> Among the beautiful names theirs is the most beautiful.
> All the glory near them passes and falls ephemerally.
> And, just as the sweet voice of a mother would,
> The voice of the nation rocks them in their tombs.

Can you imagine all the school children in their national costumes going around reciting such things? One really understands why The

To Whom It May Concern

Republic lost the war and was occupied for so many years. One also understands why Sarah smiles cynically when she recites these words to herself. She wonders: how could she have been raised on such insipidity? Did her father, her mother, her brothers die for the country in the torture chambers of the deportation zones? If so, don't they deserve that the people who sent them there come and pray at their tombs? But where are these tombs?

Sarah wonders if her cousin also remembers the poems he had to memorize when he was a boy. She must ask him. It'll be fun to find out how much he remembers, and laugh with him at all the stupidities they were fed when they were children. And yet, sometimes when Sarah translates those words in her mind into the new language she has learned in her adopted country they seem to gain powerful relevance to her feelings about this new place, and especially about Yossi who risks his life everyday for the country. The words of the poem sound almost right in that language.

She must ask her cousin if he knows that poem ... Why is his plane delayed? Is something wrong? Has she not waited long enough to see him again? In the arrival hall of the airport Sarah looks up at the TV monitor. FLIGHT 801 -- Delayed. Why is she so nervous ... so anxious?

Meanwhile at the other airport, Sarah's cousin continues to replay what happened on the day of the great round-up.

Families were being herded into the square from all the surrounding streets and being loaded on the trucks. Sarah recognized many of them. Friends of her parents. Neighbors with whom her mother talked when she went shopping. Even some of the shopkeepers. The butcher was there too with his family. Sarah was surprised because he never left his shop. She also recognized clients of her father, though lately few of them brought him shoes to repair. A girl she knew from school waved at Sarah from one of the trucks. She was wearing her winter coat, even though it was a hot day. Sarah didn't understand why all these people were wearing overcoats. Some of the women even had on their best fur coats and hats. Something about this gathering did not make sense to her.

In the center of the square crowded with the trucks, the soldiers, and the people being taken away, the neighbor woman suddenly stopped and said: you know, I wouldn't be surprised if your parents were still here in one of these trucks. Let's look for them. Yes, I bet they've been here since this morning worrying about you.

Still holding Sarah's hand, the woman rushed from truck to truck peering into each to see if by chance Sarah's parents were inside. It was hard to see anything in the big canvas-covered trucks because so many people were packed into them. The woman kept calling out the name of Sarah's parents in a loud screechy voice. She seemed impatient now. After a moment of muttering inside the grayness of the truck, someone would call out, nobody here by that name. Or someone else would ask, who is it you're looking for? The whole situation was so casual. To Sarah it seemed as though all these people with their suitcases and bags were going on vacation somewhere. She could not detect the fear and anguish in their eyes and in their gestures as they were pushed up into the trucks. There were no protests, no loud sobs, no screams. Sarah even thought that perhaps the people in the neighborhood had decided to have a huge picnic and the soldiers and police were simply helping them get organized. Some of them were even carrying blankets. But that seemed natural to Sarah. People always bring blankets when they go on a picnic. Maybe it was a picnic for Freedom Day, and her mother had forgotten to tell her.

Raymond Federman

The woman kept rushing from truck to truck. She was becoming more and more frantic, and was pulling harder on the little girl's hand, but Sarah's family was not to be found. After a while the neighbor said in an irritated voice, I suppose some of the trucks must have already left.

As Sarah and the woman approached a line of people waiting next to one of the trucks, an old woman wearing a moth-eaten fur coat that smelled of naphtha grabbed her and squeezed her in her arms. It was the grandmother of one of Sarah's school friends, but Sarah did not see her friend nearby. Ah my poor poor baby, my poor little Sarah, she stammered. Sarah felt on her cheek the hair on the old woman's wrinkled chin, and smelled the mothballs in the coat. She pulled away from her. Two soldiers lifted the old woman up onto the truck.

Further around the square, while the neighbor inspected another truck, Sarah freed her hand and drifted away to talk to the little girl who lived in the building next to hers and with whom she often played. Where is everybody going? Sarah asked.

The other girl shrugged her shoulders in a gesture of ignorance. I don't know. They didn't say. They just said we shouldn't worry, but we

56

should bring warm clothes. Maybe they're taking us to a place where it's cold. To the mountains for a vacation, yes maybe that's where we're going. They wouldn't let me take any of my dolls though, not even the one your mother made that blue dress for, they said it was not practical to take dolls. So instead I brought my yoyo just to have something to play with. And the little girl, perhaps a year younger than Sarah, big dark eyes, pulled her yoyo out of her coat pocket and proudly showed it to Sarah. Then she asked, which is your truck? Sarah did not answer, she didn't have a truck. She looked at the yoyo for a moment and then said, I've got to go, and walked away.

While Sarah was standing with her friend, the woman had approached one of the policemen. Oh no, I'm not one of these people! I'm ... I'm just a neighbor. But I have this little girl with me who was left behind. Yes she is one of them ... that's her over there. I don't know what to do with her. You see, it's impossible for me to keep her. I mean, Sir, you understand ... My husband and I ... we don't want to cause problems ... Maybe you can take her along in your truck and when you get where you're going you can help her find her parents.

The policeman shook his head. No I can't do that, Madam, I just can't. You see, I have my list and I'm responsible only for the names on this list. If we start taking extra people it'll make a mess of the whole thing. The paperwork will get confused. And it's already complicated enough. And besides, we have strict orders. You understand, Madam, we don't even have enough trucks for all these people. The best thing to do, I mean, I don't see any other way, we all have to cooperate, is for you to take this little girl directly to headquarters. They'll know what to do with her there. You know where it is, don't you? It's not far from here, just a few blocks.

The woman tried to insist. Yes yes I know where it is, but it's just that, I mean, I thought it'd be easier this way. Well thanks anyway officer, she finally said visibly annoyed as she walked to Sarah, took her hand and led her off the square. Ah what a mess, what an incredible mess. I tell you it's terrible the way they are handling this thing, the woman mumbled, not really talking directly to the child.

They were approaching the police station when suddenly Sarah jerked her hand out of the woman's grasp and started to run. Hey, where you going? Come back, come back here, the woman shouted. You're crazy. They'll catch you? But then she shrugged her shoulders in a gesture of indifference.

To Whom It May Concern

Whether or not Sarah was aware of what she was doing is hard to know. Even today, forty years later, she still cannot comprehend what made her pull away from that woman. Perhaps in her nine year old mind she vaguely realized that whatever the consequences, she could not let herself be taken to the police. That much she knew and understood, by instinct.

Even though Sarah and her brothers, like many of the other children in their neighborhood, were no longer allowed to go to public baths, libraries, movies, swimming pools, and many other such places, it was not clear to them why it had to be so. They were never given a reason, and when their parents and relatives talked about the war, they did so in hushed voices in some foreign language the children had never learned. Much of what the adults discussed or lamented was always whispered, so that Sarah and her brothers knew nothing. Don't ask questions, they were told, it's better if you don't ask. Protected by this silence, Sarah had grown in total ignorance of her fate. Yet at that moment, however insignificant she was, as the neighbor led her by the hand, she understood that she could not let herself be taken to the police. No, she could not go there. And besides, since her mother and father and her brothers were not in the trucks on the square, then maybe they had been sent home, yes maybe the police made a mistake and told them to go home, and they were waiting in the apartment, worrying because she had not returned from the bakery, thinking maybe she had been in an accident.

While running Sarah convinced herself that her parents were home, that the whole morning had been a mistake, a bad dream. Just before turning the corner of the street she stopped and glanced behind her. The woman had disappeared. She must have gone inside the police station. Sarah was breathing hard, her chest heaving uncontrollably. The strap of one of her sandals was torn. Suddenly Sarah broke out into sobs. She stood a moment rubbing her eyes with the back of her hand, but soon she started running again, holding the torn sandal in her hand. She turned into a side street to avoid the square with the trucks. All the streets were deserted now, and many windows had their shutters closed. Even the stores had their grates pulled shut like on Sunday. Sarah finally reached the street where she lived. It too was empty. She raced up the three flights of stairs and banged on the door of her apartment, calling out. No one answered. She was not crying now. She knocked again with both fists. She knew she shouldn't stay here long. The woman next door would soon return with the police. Finally she ran down the stairs, but stopped at the street entrance. Her body was shaking. She stuck her head out of the door and looked on both sides to see if the woman was coming. There was no one in the street except for a dog, the butcher's big black dog who was barking at the closed door of the butcher shop. Sarah rushed into the street and ran, away from the dog and from the square.

She knew her way around these ancient streets. She had often played there after school with her brothers and friends. Several of her aunts and uncles lived in the neighborhood. She knew those streets by heart. When she reached the main avenue lined with the glorious historic monuments she stopped at the curb as if waiting to cross the wide street on her way to some errand. Cars and army trucks were rushing by. She was still trembling a little and breathing heavily but trying to hold her body still so no one would notice. She had no idea where to go, what to do, yet knew she had to get away from this neighborhood.

Standing on the edge of the sidewalk, facing the traffic, her body stiff with fear, Sarah suddenly brought her hand to her chest and covered the patch sewn on her dress. She had forgotten about it. Slowly her fingers made a claw and she ripped the patch off. It made a hole in her dress, right above her heart. She thought how angry her mother would be that she tore her dress. From the day her mother had sewn those ugly patches on all her clothes they felt like giant insects gnawing and scratching at her chest. She crumpled the piece of yellow cloth and extending her arm close to her body as far down as she could she let it drop in the gutter. She turned around to see if anyone had noticed. The street was busy, and there were a lot soldiers in the crowd, but no one was paying attention to the little girl.

She had been so ashamed of that patch since the day, two years ago, when her mother told the children they had to wear one of these on all their clothes. Sarah and her brothers wanted to know why, why they had to wear this thing. But when their mother -- a gentle self- sacrificing woman -- started to cry quietly they stopped asking for an explanation. Often when Sarah went out, even during the summer, she would wear a long scarf around her neck and let one end fall loosely over the patch. Her mother had shown her how to do this. You just let it hang there. You're not really hiding it, and it looks nice this way.

Sarah started walking away from where she lived. She wanted to run. When she reached the circle with the fountain made of giant monsters spouting water, where all the main avenues intersect, she remembered that her Aunt Basha lived nearby, down one of these streets. Maybe she was home? Maybe the police hadn't been to her house? She must go and tell her what happened. Aunt Basha will know what to do.

To Whom It May Concern

Sarah knew that her Uncle Joseph had left the city a few days ago, but that Aunt Basha had stayed behind. The old aunt explained to Sarah and her brothers when they visited last Saturday that their uncle had taken the boys for a vacation in the country.

For weeks already rumors had been circulating in the neighborhood about the possible round-up, but since in the past only men were taken, Sarah's uncle had made plans to get away with his two sons. In those days there were many ways one could buy information and even survival. Aunt Basha and Uncle Joseph were rich. The poor always get dispatched first in a war, it's an old truth. They die of ignorance and want.

Every Saturday Sarah and her brothers visited Aunt Basha, their mother's older sister, even though the children didn't like her. She was mean, old, ugly and fat. She had red blotches on her face, and purple veins in her legs. She made Sarah cut the hair in her ears and in her nose with a little pair of scissors, and she yelled at the children for making too much noise when they played games. And also Aunt Basha's sons, Roger and Robert, liked to tease their younger cousins. But on Saturdays Aunt Basha would prepare a big meal with meat. It was hard to get meat then, but Basha was rich and she knew all about the black market. On Saturday she also baked cakes. Sometimes she would make a package with the left-overs for the children to take home, but if Sarah's father saw the food he would get angry and scream, I don't need her charity, and he would throw the package into the garbage.

Yes Sarah must go and tell Aunt Basha what happened. Tell her about the people on the square, about the police and the soldiers and the trucks. Basha will know what to do. She'll know where to find Sarah's parents. And then everything will be fine. Yes just like it was before. And maybe the whole family can go away together to the country until the end of the war ...

That's what they all told themselves, the parents as well as the children, even while being hurled into the great void. After the war everything will be fine again, just like before.

Sarah was walking quickly now. In the distance she could see the tall building where her aunt lived. As she approached she saw her coming out into the street. She was wearing her fur coat and dragging an enormous suitcase toward the curb where a taxi was waiting. It was really Aunt Basha, Sarah recognized her funny cossack hat. Sarah ran toward the taxi waving her arms and calling to her, but just as she reached the taxi the door slammed shut. Aunt Basha saw her because she waved and made a face as though explaining something through the rear window of the car as it pulled away. Sarah stood there puzzled, not comprehending why her aunt left so quickly without even asking what she was doing here all alone.

It took the entire day, that July 16, from early morning till late into the night, for all the people in the neighborhood who were on the lists to be rounded up. The news of the arrests was spreading quickly. A few who had the money and somewhere to go managed to escape. The others simply waited to be taken. Aunt Basha, who rarely left her apartment, probably just learned that women and children were also being arrested, and quickly packed all she could in that huge suitcase -- her clothes, her jewelry, all the silver around the house, and of course her money. The banknotes she kept hidden under the mattress of her bed. Yes that's where she kept money. When the children went to visit their aunt, she would sometimes give each of them a small bill to buy a little something. As they stood by the door ready to leave, she would tell the children, wait here, and she would disappear into the bedroom, but Sarah and her brothers once saw through the half-open door how the old aunt reached under the mattress to take out the bills.

65

Raymond Federman

Sarah stood at the curb wondering if Basha's gesture meant goodbye or something else. Maybe she was saying to Sarah wait here, I'll be back for you. Everything was so confusing. Again tears welled up in her eyes. She moved close to the building and turned toward the wall so the people in the street would not see her cry. She waited a long time, but Aunt Basha did not return.

After a while Sarah stopped crying. Her eyes were red and puffy. She started walking aimlessly with her head down, looking at her feet. Her body was leading her, but suddenly she realized she was on her way home. She stopped. No ... no she mustn't go there. She turned around and walked in the opposite direction.

For several hours Sarah wandered in the city, but never too far from her neighborhood, as if waiting for a prearranged moment to return home and resume her safe life with her family. Her body was calm now. She even stopped a few times to look at shopwindows. Her mind had closed itself to the urgency of the moment, it could neither backtrack to what had happened that morning nor could it project forward to what awaited her later when it would be dark and she would find herself alone in the streets.

To Whom It May Concern

It was late afternoon now. Sarah's steps had led her to the street her mother told the children never to go alone. She recognized the street because when the three children went for their visits to Aunt Basha, Sarah's brothers would sometimes make a detour through this street even if it was longer this way. The children always went to Basha without their parents because Sarah's father had had a fight with her, about money, and he never went to their house and didn't even let Sarah's mother go there. Since they were on their own the boys would insist on making that detour even though they knew their mother would be furious if she found out.

Simon and Benjamin would drag their little sister there to show her the beautiful women who walked in the street or stood in doorways. Dressed in fancy clothes, with lots of shimmering jewels, and colorful make-up on their faces, they looked like they were going to a party. They seemed so joyful to Sarah, always joking with the people who passed by.

Sarah couldn't understand why her brothers kept giggling behind their hands. You're so stupid, so stupid, Simon would say to Sarah. And if you tell Mamma we came this way you'll really get it. I'll smack you! Simon was thirteen, Benjamin ten at the time. I'll beat you up too,

67

Benjamin would repeat after his older brother, though he too didn't understand why these women were standing around in the street.

Sarah stepped off the curb to walk around four women who were blocking the narrow sidewalk. They were wearing tight shiny dresses that reached way above their knees. One of them shouted at Sarah, hey little girl, aren't you a bit young to be walking the streets? The other women laughed, and Sarah burst into tears. Hey what's wrong? Why the tears suddenly? asked the woman who had spoken to Sarah. Come here, come here little one and tell me why you're crying. Sarah hesitated, but the woman had already approached her and was wiping her cheeks with the large perfumed handkerchief she had taken out of her bosom. Are you lost?

Sarah's face became disorganized as she broke into loud sobs, but the woman's voice was so kind, so gentle, and her hands so soft, that immediately Sarah wanted to tell her everything that happened since early morning when her mother sent her to the bakery. She tried, but the words remained caught in her throat.

Come now, stop that, you're a big girl, the woman said making her voice sound harder than it really was. Here blow your nose and tell me what's wrong. A pretty little girl like you shouldn't be crying, it'll make your eyes all red.

Still crying, but quietly now, Sarah managed to stammer in one long breath, it's my mother and my father ... and my brothers too ... they ... they were taken away ... this morning ... I don't know where they are ... and there were all these people and all these soldiers on the square and trucks ... and this woman ... this woman she lives next to us in the same building ... she ... she wanted to take me ...

Did you run away? The woman asked. She was pretty. She was not really like any other women Sarah knew, she looked more like ... like an older sister. She wasn't really a woman, more like a girl. She had long straight reddish hair, lots of black around her green eyes, and she was wearing a tight purple dress with gold trim around the neck. Her lips were painted purple. Sarah thought she was the most beautiful girl she had ever seen, even more beautiful than the movie stars in the pictures her brothers hid inside their schoolbooks. And she was so nice, she spoke so gently.

No I didn't run away. Sarah had calmed down now. After she blew her nose in the handkerchief, she explained to the girl, and to the other three who had gathered around her, how she was at the bakery when the soldiers came. I was not home. They forgot me. My mother and my father, they forgot me.

Forgot you! You lucky girl. You don't know how lucky you are. Like everyone else, the women knew very well what was happening. The girl with the purple dress took Sarah's hand and pulled her into a doorway. Come with me, quick, maybe we can fix things. A man in shirtsleeves wearing suspenders and a felt hat came out into the corridor. The girl spoke with him in a low voice. Sarah couldn't hear what they were saying. Then the girl in purple took Sarah up the narrow stairs to a room on the third floor. It was a beautiful room. All purple and gold. The same colors as the girl's dress. The walls, the curtains, the bed cover, the rug on the floor, everything was purple with gold, except for the bright red dress of the big doll propped against pillows at the head of the bed. It was the most beautiful room Sarah had ever seen. It was not like a real room but like a room in a storybook or in a movie or in a dream. There was a tall mirror, also framed in gold, on the wall facing the bed, and next to the mirror, on a little square table, a washbasin with blue flowers painted on it.

What's your name? the young woman asked as she locked the door.

To Whom It May Concern

Sarah.

Sarah! Oh that's a beautiful name. Mine is Josette but everybody calls me Jojo. You can call me Jojo too if you like. Look don't be afraid, we'll take care of you. Everything will be fine. I'm sure your mother and father will be back soon. You just have to wait here until we find out what happened. Okay?

Sarah was still standing by the door. She was not scared now. She knew everything would be fine because this room was so beautiful.

Josette went to the window and closed the curtains. It's better if you don't go near the window. Okay. Are you hungry? Do you want something to eat?

Sarah hesitated. No I ate this morning. The woman, she gave me some food.

You're sure? Josette insisted. You must be hungry if you haven't eaten anything since this morning.

Sarah started to cry again. Sniffling and wiping her eyes she tried to explain how the woman ... she wanted to take me ... she said the police would find them ...

Don't cry, please don't cry. You can tell me all that later. But first you must calm down. All right! Josette made Sarah sit on the edge of the bed and again wiped the tears with her handkerchief. I'm sure you must be hungry, she said. She went to the door unlocked it and called down the stairs, hey Gugusse!

Yeah, what's up, a man shouted from downstairs.

Bring something up for the little girl to eat, anything you have down there. Bread, some cheese maybe, a glass of milk. Josette then turned to Sarah. Now listen carefully. You're going to stay here in this room. You can sit on that chair to eat, and when you're finished you can lie down on the bed to rest. I'm going to go out, just for a short time. To talk to some people about you, some friends. Maybe they can find out what happened to your family. Don't worry, we'll take care of you. We'll find a place for you until your parents come back. You won't be scared to stay here alone? Right? You're a big girl. I'll be back soon. Josette passed her fingers gently through Sarah's hair.

To Whom It May Concern

No I'm not scared, Sarah said, but ... she hesitated ... I have to go ... I have to go to the bathroom.

Josette smiled. She bent down and pulled out a chamber pot from under the bed. Here you can use this.

Sarah blushed.

Ah come on, don't be shy, Josette said as she handed Sarah the chamber pot, here take it over there in that corner and I'll close my eyes.

Sarah carried the chamber pot to the other side of the bed, pulled her panties down to her ankles, crouched holding her dress taut across her back so as not to wet it. Josette held one hand over her eyes, but smiled when she heard the loud trickling.

The man called Gugusse brought a loaf of bread with some cheese, an apple, and a bottle of milk. Josette moved the washbasin off the table. She sliced the bread and the cheese. Sit down here and eat now, she said. Eat slowly. And to Gugusse still standing by the door looking at the little girl, handing him the chamber pot, here empty this downstairs.

While Sarah was chewing a piece of bread with cheese, Josette gave her a loud kiss on the cheek. You're a pretty little thing you know. How old are you. Ten? Eleven?

No, I'm nine years old.

Only nine! Josette shook her head, only nine, she repeated in a whisper. Suddenly she noticed the hole in Sarah's dress. How did you do that? What happened to your dress?

Sarah looked away from Josette, her cheeks flushed as she said, her mouth full of food, I tore the patch off. Josette stroked Sarah's hair, then she bent down and gave her another kiss on the cheek. Look, I'm going to try and find out what happened to your family. I don't know where, but I'm going to try. What's your last name?

Sarah told Josette her last name.

To Whom It May Concern

All right, I'll see what I can do. You stay here. Okay! I'm going to lock the door behind me so no one can come in. You won't be able to open it from inside, but that's all right. I won't be long.

Sarah heard the key turn twice in the lock. She got up from the table and went to listen behind the door. There was no sound in the staircase now. She tiptoed back to the table. The wooden floor creaked under the purple rug. She didn't dare walk all the way to the window to look outside in the street, but she could hear voices coming from below. As she reached for a piece of bread on the table she caught sight of herself in the mirror on the wall. It startled her. She didn't recognize the skinny body and the disheveled face she saw in the full-length mirror. It felt as if a stranger was in the room with her, a homely little girl she had never seen before. The hair was all messed, the eyes red and puffy, and the dress dirty and torn. But when the girl's hand in the mirror moved toward the hole in the dress, Sarah realized it was her hand and her dress, and that she had made that hole. Standing there disoriented and alone, Sarah didn't cry, she just stared at the mirror, memorizing herself while the black clouds of uncertainty gathered outside the room, just beyond her still unspoiled future. Covering the hole on her chest with her hand, Sarah thought how angry her mother would be because her dress was torn, but she would explain how it happened, how she thought it would be better to take the patch off. Her mother would understand, yes she would, and she would say to her, it's all right, it's all right, my little love.

Sarah turned away from the mirror and sat on the edge of the bed, her skinny legs dangling. She was sleepy now. Her head felt heavy. The bed was soft and the cover silky and smooth. The big doll propped at the head of the bed with her plump shiny legs spread apart had one arm raised as if reaching for Sarah. The red dress had a white lace collar, and the black patent shoes were fastened with buttons. The doll had blue eyes and very blonde hair tied with a big red bow. Her mouth was slightly open as if trying to speak to Sarah. She looked so real and so pretty, Sarah almost spoke to the doll. After a while she curled up on the bed, pulled the doll next to her and put her arms around it. The doll's smooth shiny skin felt cool against Sarah's arms. Soon Sarah was asleep, and the doll too closed her eyes ...

That's how I see it so far. It's taking shape. I feel like I'm on the verge of a huge saga. Lots of problems to solve but I'm beginning to get a sense of the story. It's not going to be easy. I can already hear the objections, but remember, writing a book is also learning how to write a book. The difficulty will be to keep track of everything, not only the past and the present, but the future too. If only one could inscribe simultaneously in the same sentence different moments of the story. Create a stereophonic effect. That's how it feels right now inside my skull. Voices within voices entangled in their own fleeting garrulousness.

I'll stop here, with Sarah asleep in the purple den, asleep on the bed where I suppose hundreds of men have made love to Josette, even perhaps enemy soldiers. Little Sarah asleep in that perfumed room of pleasure with the chubby doll in her arms and confused dreams in her head.

What do you think of Josette? She's gorgeous, you know, with her youthful freckles, her voracious mouth, her mischievous sensuality. Seductive without being the ultimate gaping fatality. She is much younger than Sarah realizes. Eighteen or nineteen. Do you also get aroused by your characters? I get all worked up just looking at Josette. The kind-hearted whore. A bit stereotyped, but what the hell. The problem is that I don't know what to do with her. Who knows, maybe Josette the prostitute will turn into a saint, like in the good old tales, and the whole thing will become mystical.

We'll see. Meanwhile write to me. Make suggestions. Object. What's the use having a buddy like you if one cannot rely on him. And tell me more about what you're doing these days. So long.

To Whom It May Concern

Pearl Harbor Day. Here we celebrate this occasion, because it's also our daughter's birthday. A memorable day. Where were you, back then, when the Japanese caught the Americans with their pants down and sent a good many of them into eternity. Do you remember? Me, I vaguely recall, I was up to my innocent crotch in the sordid confusion of puberty, unconscious to the world in spite of the great war raging around me. And Sarah? Little cousin Sarah. She had not yet entered the dark tunnel of her misfortune, but it loomed ahead of her, inescapable and threatening.

Pearl Harbor Day! Did you know that it was also on a December 7 that mass extermination began at Chelmno. Yes, our daughter was born on that historical date. A Sagittarius. Smart but stubborn. She's home from the big city for the occasion. It's good to have her around for a few days. All grown-up suddenly. So independent and so argumentative. She loves to tease her old man. (By the way, did I mention that Sarah's cousin, the sculptor, also has a daughter about the same age as ours?)

I showed her the new shoes I just bought. Big heavy clumsy yellow things that come up over the ankles. Workmen's shoes. It's winter now. No, not the season of comfort, Rimbaud had it all wrong, the season of discomfort. I need these to trample in the slush, I tried to explain. The kid laughed. Pop, they're atrocious! They look like orthopedic shoes. Children have such a way of making the folks feel good, don't they? You too can laugh. But wait till your kids reach the age of smart-aleck reasoning.

During the birthday festivities, a few hours ago (and what a meal! -- ah what a splendid cook my wife is, besides everything else -- escargots, filet mignon à la sauce béarnaise, champignons, crème caramel for dessert, you know, the real French thing, with a superb bottle of St. Emilion), the daughter asks what I'm working on.

To Whom It May Concern

Oh nothing much, I mumble. Just thinking about something, but I don't have it yet. I don't see the shape of it.

The wife, while pouring the coffee: Pop is going to write a serious book this time. Can you believe that? As if all the others had been game-playing.

A serious book! Him --? It's the daughter, with a look of astonishment on her face. She's so beautiful when she puts on the puzzled look. Mom, you really think Pop will ever be capable of writing something serious? Personally, I like him better when he's funny and preposterous.

Then to me: what's it about Pop?

Since she's interested, I tell her what I've already told you about the Sarah book. How the two cousins, survivors of the unforgivable enormity, are going to be reunited in a far away place after years of separation. The daughter shakes her head in approval. Sounds great, Pop! Suddenly the birthday cake tastes magnificent. If she doesn't

Raymond Federman

object, that's fifty percent of the battle won. After all it is for her, unadmittedly, that the stuff is being written.

I think I'm on the verge of a great tale, I say. Something really big and profound.

Oh wow! the lovely daughter sneers. But later, as I am telling how Sarah's son Yossi is in charge of the special task force chasing the terrorists who bombed the bus, she asks if this business with the terrorists is going to turn this book into a wild adventure story. That would be neat, she says with teasing enthusiasm, lots of international intrigue, lots of action, twisted plots and counterplots. What fun. Guys shooting each other all over the place. And maybe you can have Sarah's cousin get involved.

I know she's only kidding, but I protest. Look, it's not what I have in mind. And besides, I don't know what to do with Yossi. I don't know how he fits into the story. I would like a character like him -- someone tough and dedicated to symbolize the new generation in Sarah's adopted country.

To Whom It May Concern

Well, let's see what we can do with him, the kid says all excited, and for the fun of it she starts exploring possibilities. All of a sudden she cries out, I got it, I got it! Yossi is taken prisoner. The terrorists have him stashed away in a hideout somewhere in the mountains, you know, in a remote section of the country, and they are torturing him. A rescue team is formed and Sarah's cousin goes along. I know that sounds farfetched since he's only a visitor in that country, but we can always invent a reason why they let him go on this mission. Maybe when he was a young man he was a commando, or something, and he had special training for this kind of stuff. And he's still in great shape for his age. Right? ... I got it, you could have him be a paratrooper, like you were Pop when you were in the army. I mean, when the cousin was younger. After all, isn't he modeled on you?

Hey wait a minute, this is not what I have in mind. I don't really want to get involved with terrorism. I threw in that business of the bus just to give a sense of how that country exists in the midst of constant threats of destruction. That's all I wanted to suggest. I am not interested in violence, or international conflicts. I just want to write something simple about two people tormented by their past, and anguished about the state of their present life. That's all. I want to show how human beings confront their failures even though in the eyes of others they appear to have made a success. You don't need violence for that, and certainly not a plot.

Ah come on Pop, it'll be boring if you don't put in some action. After all you have the perfect stuff. The terrorists. The bombing of the bus. Torture.

She almost has me convinced, and for a moment I visualize the whole scene. The cousin infiltrates the terrorist camp and he's the one who saves Yossi. There's a shoot out, and the two of them escape in a tank, or in a helicopter. Not bad! Later, when they are safe, Sarah cries as she embraces her son and her cousin.

And you know what, Pop, you could make a fortune with a book like that. For sure it would become a movie. That would be something. We would be rich suddenly. You could buy me an apartment in the city, and you and Mom could take a trip around the world. Well, we'll see. Anyway, I haven't even begun to write. I'm only thinking about the story. Getting ready for it. The whole thing might turn into a disaster.

To Whom It May Concern

So it goes in our family. Helps the morale though to have such lively discussions. The kid is leaving in the morning. Back to the big city to go on being a waitress in some dive before becoming the great whatever she will be. She's saving money to go to Africa. She wants to see how things are in the heart of darkness. She cares. She cares about people -- the people of this world. When she was in college her grandmother once asked what she was majoring in, and she answered: The World! She's leaving in the morning.

It's the middle of the night now and I can't sleep. The house is quiet. Everybody's asleep, even Sam on his private carpet, dreaming of bones I suppose, or bitches. Do you know that the little guy, twelve years old now, never had a piece of ass as far as I know. He's been so fenced in. I wish there were dog bordellos, I would take him there for a spin and give him the time of his doglife.

Your last reply irritated me. It didn't give me anything to work with. It was so evasive. You seem to refuse to commit yourself when you say: I know you're anxious about a true response, and I'll give you what I have, but you also know how disposed, predisposed I am to your work.

Raymond Federman

Look, I am not asking for kindness and civility. I thought we were beyond that kind of stuff, beyond the non-committal response. Give me honest brutality. What really burns me is when you come up with this: I hear you largely, you say, it's a sort of music I'm in tune with, so I suppose my pleasure overwhelms my judgment ...

What kind of crap is this! Why can't you be as critical as anyone else? Why does it prejudice the case to ask for your opinion? I'm not asking that you do for this one the intimate things you've done for the other books, it's too early for that, but I need a push. I need your crutches until I am able to walk alone. So I'll keep bugging you, hoping that you are listening, and then, if all goes well, perhaps I'll manage to write myself off as a loss.

You see, I'm convinced that we must now move beyond mere fables, beyond the neatly packaged stories which provide a chain of terminal satisfactions from predictable beginnings to foreshadowed endings. We have come so far in the long journey of literature that all the stories whisper the same old thing to us in the same cracked voice. And so we must dig in to see where raw words and fundamental sounds are buried so that the great silence within can finally be decoded.

To Whom It May Concern

I have a feeling I'm repeating something I said to you, or you to me, when you were struggling with those vain repetitions of yours. Those monsters you were trying to tame. Here the beasts are still roaming wild in my brain and aren't ready to be locked up in the book cage. Not ready for paper domestication. I offer myself dates for the confrontation. For the entrance into the cage. It was to have been December first, and here we are nearly Christmas and I have postponed till January first. Yes why not begin with the new year. Seems like a logical point of departure. So let's leave it at that.

It's late now, almost morning, everything is getting blurred in my head. But for future reference try to keep in mind where I left Sarah and her cousin.

The cousin stranded at the airport of the city where he was born, ruminating old memories, his plane delayed by a few hours. And Sarah, the nine year old little girl, forgotten in the great war. Remember? When we left her she had just fallen asleep in Josette's room, her arms wrapped around a plastic doll. I hope she doesn't wake up before I am ready for her.

Meanwhile the cousin waits. Unable to concentrate on the book he is reading, he lets his mind wander. What would he have become if he had gone with Sarah to the desert thirty-five years ago instead of seeking fame and fortune elsewhere? What would he be today? Just a farmer like her? Certainly not a sculptor, an artist clinging to a vanishing reputation. These are the questions he has asked himself over the years. He often tried to imagine Sarah's life. He has always been fascinated by the desert, has always thought of himself as a nomad. He even calls himself a nomad. That word alone brings to his mind images of unbearable heat, burning sand, and boundlessness. How often he has awakened from a dream in which he saw himself walking away into the desert, gradually disappearing into the sand. Or else saw, in that dream, a solitary figure slowly rising toward him from far away across the expanse of sand until he recognized his own face in that man, but never realizing when he awoke that he had traveled through eternity.

He tries to remember the name of the place where Sarah lives. The word is on the tip of his tongue but he cannot find it.

In the language of this land, Sarah will explain to her cousin after he arrives and she takes him around the camp farm, Groulote means

To Whom It May Concern

outpost because it is right on the border. In the early days, even after we stopped our enemies and forced them back into their own country, we were attacked almost every night. Ours was more like an army post than a farm. We all took turns standing guard at night. Even me. I was only fifteen when I arrived.

One night ... Sarah will hesitate, her voice fading into silence, her pale gray eyes staring at something her cousin will not be able to see in the darkness of that distant night, and then after a long pause she will speak again, quickly, breathlessly ... One night a figure appeared in front of me just a few feet away, holding a gun. I was sure it was a gun though it was hard to see. He came out of the dark, and stood before me like a huge shadow. I got scared, I couldn't see very well. I was all alone. I had a revolver and I pulled it out of the holster. I was trembling so much I had to hold it with both hands. When the figure moved closer I shot. I shot. The bullet struck him in the face. In the mouth. His blood spurted out on me, all over my clothes, and I screamed ... Still staring into the darkness of that night, Sarah will continue in a whisper... He was lying on the ground all curled up, groaning like a wounded animal. Then he stopped moving. I became hysterical. I was scream-ing and crying. Elie and some of the other men from the camp rushed to where I was and covered the body with a coat and took me away. Ssh, they kept saying, ssh. They led me inside a room and made me lie down on a cot. Elie sat next to me to comfort me. For three days I was totally delirious. Before they covered the body I saw the face in the glare of the flashlights. It was all torn, but I could tell he was very young. Just a boy. About my age. Maybe even younger. I don't really know if he had a gun. I never wanted to ask Elie. We were not married then, Elie and I. We got married later, when I turned twenty. Elie and I never talk about what happened that night ... I know he was just a boy ... He looked a lot like Yossi, like my son Yossi ...

There'll be no tears in Sarah's eyes when she'll tell that story to her cousin. Just a look of profound sadness on her face. Her pale gray eyes still staring into the distance, she will recall how terrified she had been that night, but surprised too by the simplicity of death. Then after a long silence Sarah will add, her voice now clear and ardent, do you know that we had to walk forty kilometers in the desert carrying bags of water on our backs so we could start growing things here. We didn't have trucks then. Nothing. Only our hands and a few tools. And of course our guns.

Sitting at the airport, the cousin tries to imagine what life on that outpost might be like. He visualizes a group of people living together in wooden shacks who work hard all day to make vegetables grow out of the sand and then gather around campfires in the twilight to sing and dance. The perfect pastoral life. He is aware that these are naive notions, but for him that place is just a set of colorful and exotic images. What one sees in the movies or on postcards and travel posters. He knows so little about the life there, about the people, the politics, the history. Sarah's letters never really said much about all that. Her letters spoke mostly of her husband and her children. He tried over the years to become interested in that country's fragile existence, its successes and failures, but from a distance, by reading books and articles in magazines, without any real serious commitment. Without any great passion. Will he be disappointed? Or will he fall in love with that land? How often he's been told of its beauty and seductiveness. Or will he hate it? Hate what that country stands for. Its contradictory politics, its restrictive laws, its obtuse views of religion. But why is he so concerned suddenly?

All his life he felt he belonged in the world, on the battlefield, with real people, but instead he spent most of it locked in a room struggling with images. Why is he so apprehensive? Perhaps because of the show at the museum.

Raymond Federman

He wonders if his sculptures have arrived safely. Fifty-two pieces. A large part of his life's work. They were shipped weeks ago. He watched at the pier when the crates were loaded. What will they think of his work? It all happened so quickly, the invitation from the museum, as if they had just discovered him. Why this sudden interest? Did they see something in his work relevant to their lives? What can those grotesque things he makes have to do with their problems? His sculptures often reach into abstraction. They do not reflect reality but the crumbling of reality in the mind. His aim is not so much to comfort or celebrate as to confront and disturb. There is nothing elegant or delicate about his method. It is violent and irrational. He doesn't romance the stone, he mugs it. He is not interested in establishing an easy accommodation with his material when he sculpts, nor interested in self-defense. No, he invades the material to destroy it. He wonders if they'll ask why there are no sculptures from the last five years? Well he could say it was a decision he made at the last moment not to include his recent work because he's been trying new things. They might insist. Will he have to explain, justify those last five years of nothing? Nothing! The great gap into which he has fallen. The paralysis of thinking rather than working.

Some five years ago, at the peak of his fame, when his work was sought and admired, he became obsessed with the absolute truth of shapes and contours, and began to meditate on his art. This led him to doubt his own work. Slowly he sank into despair as he compared the immensity of his hopes with the sudden revelation of how limited his resources were. Arguing with himself that reality did not exist because truth could not be reproduced, he convinced himself that sculpture only creates lifeless geometric figures. This transfiguration prevented him from doing any new work, though he pretended to be working. The pieces he presented were not even sculpted, but found rocks artfully displayed. Huge boulders, untouched and uncut, representing nothing but themselves, as if the stone refused to let forms come out.

His head full of doubt, his body in panic, he seemed to have lost his strength, to have become helpless. Dragging himself from day to day, hardly getting out into the world, lying in bed late into the morning, shuffling about the house in torn slippers or sitting in a chair facing the wall listening to his heart beat, perhaps wishing that it would stop, he became absent from himself. Five years went by before he began to feel the return of energy and hope. Then one day the invitation from the museum in Sarah's country came. He was pleased though puzzled by this sudden interest. He accepted to be present for the opening. This way it would give him a chance to see Sarah after so many years.

Raymond Federman

Excuse me, Sir, would you like a little more coffee? It's the airline attendant jostling him out of his reverie. She is in front of him with a pot of steaming coffee in one hand. He notices her legs. Long silky legs. Notices her hips swaying in a very tight fitting dark blue skirt. He looks up. No thanks, I ... What a lovely face. The mouth. The eyes. Big and mischievous. And her body. Exquisite proportions. He changes his mind -- oh, yes please, I'll have a cup ... sugar only -- just to have her stand there a moment longer.

Why is he feeling so down? So moody? He could be talking with the other passengers. Find out where they are from, if they have been to that country before. Instead he chose this far corner of the lounge to be alone with his thoughts, pretending to be reading.

The name tag says Cheryl. What a gorgeous creature, and what a set of boobs, he observes as he shifts from the somber thoughtful half of himself into the aggressive sensual half. How he would love to jump her bones.

I hope you're not getting too bored, Cheryl says. We should know soon when we will take off.

To Whom It May Concern

He gives her the long look. How he would love just to sit alone with her in a room. Sketch her. And then maybe. Two hours to kill. He would tell her everything about himself. Yes a sculptor. Would tell her about the exhibition of his work at the museum. She would be impressed. An artist! She's never met an artist before. They would grab each other. Just like that. They would caress and kiss with abandon. He would unbutton her blouse, ease his face away from hers and move his mouth toward her bold bare breasts. He'd lick her nipples into a state of anxious arousal. Then they would undress each other with frantic fingers. He would stroke her hips while she ran her fingernails down his back. They would collapse on the bed. On the floor. Just like that. For the mere pleasure, for the sport of it, without much talk, without questioning. To pass the time while waiting for the plane to take off. He'd push his hand between her legs. Grab her. Feel the wetness. She'd giggle. Then she'd be sitting on top of him, legs astride his chest, telling him what a nice body he has. It's because he plays a lot of tennis and golf, he'd explain. Also being a sculptor is a very physical activity. She wouldn't be able to ask what sort of statues he makes because her mouth would be full of him now, and he would let his arms drop to his sides, and enjoy the pleasure of her lips and of her tongue ...

Raymond Federman

If there is anything else I can do, Sir, just let me know, Cheryl says, still standing in front of him holding her coffee pot. He suddenly feels annoyed. He puts on the impatient traveler's voice and asks, any word about our flight?

Nothing yet Sir, Cheryl answers with a delicious smile. We're still scheduled for a five o'clock departure. That should put us at our destination around eight. We should be getting an announcement soon. Sorry about the delay. Then still wearing her smile and swaying her hips in her tight blue skirt, she moves away with her coffee pot and stops in front of another passenger.

The cousin gets up and walks around the lounge to stretch his legs. He is annoyed that the attendant kept calling him sir. After a while he returns to his corner and slouches in the seat. He feels sleepy now. He hates those night flights across the ocean. He closes his eyes. Where was I? he wonders, trying to recapture his thoughts.

And me too, where was I? I mean before I got distracted by the cousin's erotic fantasy ... Oh yes, asking you to remember where I left Sarah and her cousin. There is more to say about them, especially about the time when they were separated. Remember, after the war, the two of them, hugging each other on the train platform. Sarah fifteen now, trying not to cry as she waved goodbye. We'll have to return to that moment, and even move further back in time to see how these two children survived, each abandoned in a corner of the great war, until they found each other, and discovered they had been given an excess of life. Ah so many crossroads here. So many layers. Where shall I pick up the thread of this fable? Where?

Not tonight though. No, not tonight. It's late now. I'm tired, and you too must be tired of all this groping in the dark. But if you care to listen I will tell you more. I will tell you the whole story up to the final flash of panic. But not now. Sam just woke up. He's barking. It's already light outside. I have to take him out for a walk.

To Whom It May Concern

Wednesday, December 21

Winter is here. It hit us this morning with uncontrolled fury. We are snowed in. I am settling into the comfort of helplessness wondering if one can debate the correctness or incorrectness of the unforgivable enormity. There was something so bureaucratic about it. It was kept as a dirty grimy secret rather than being acknowledged as the product of a terrible destiny. That really troubles the mind.

This is a good day to ponder such things.

To Whom It May Concern

Monday, January 2

Well I tried. I really tried. What a mess. An early disaster. During the night, the night that ushers in the new year, the night of resolutions, a voice was counseling me. A simple clear voice told me to sit here, chain myself to my desk and get on with it. That voice told me that I should not travel, not skylark, as I have been contemplating since nothing is happening here, that I should not mess around any more, and simply consider driving myself mad with the frenzy of it.

And so up bright and early, on the first day of this new year, as promised, feeling awful, I faced the empty sheet of paper. The wife was lazing in the bedroom in her bathrobe, shouting at the dog for sniffing her panties. All day and late into the night, I sat before the old

101

machine and banged away. I even skipped all the new year's day parades and football games, and you know what a fanatic I am. Well, actually I did cheat for a couple of hours in the late afternoon to watch the gritty Huskies demolish the mighty Sooners.

So January first, all day and late into the night, I tried. Even went on with it frantically the next day, but by the middle of the afternoon I threw it all away. No good. No shape, no music to the words. So here I am, stranded again. I couldn't get hold of it. It seemed to have no purpose, no direction. It was pure chaos. Not that I fear chaos. I delight in disorder. But this time there is too much here to deal with all at once.

Besides, the language seemed so flat. Poor and thin. Empty of resonance. Another false start, that's all. What the hell, so many false starts in one's life. Let's just say it was not the right moment.

It's the opening that I can't get. The where to begin. Do I start with the cousin in the fertile land of misrepresentation, or do I start with Sarah in the barren desert? Or should it be the place in between where they were born? And why not the farm where the cousin wasted his puberty shoveling manure, or the lampshade factory where he worked after the war? I could also start on the train, on the boat that took him into exile. The plane. So many possible points of departure.

And who should speak first, or rather who should be spoken of first? Sarah? Her cousin? Sarah the little girl lost in the war? Sarah the woman-child learning to share with her cousin the anxieties of survival? Or should it be the middle-aged cousin contemplating his failures, or younger struggling to achieve his vocation. Or else Sarah asleep in Josette's room on the edge of incomprehension? Or Sarah waiting anxiously for the arrival of her famous cousin while looking at her many selves through the keyhole of memory? So many angles here. This is not plane geometry, this is trigonometry.

The best thing to do now is wait, and hope that while speculating I'll stumble on the right design. Meanwhile this salutary reprieve I spent in front of the typewriter was, at least for a couple of days, the only thing that stood between me and despair. Now the typewriter is mute again, but it has a new ribbon, just in case.

Perhaps to avoid the issue of where -- where to begin and where to go, I should pull the old trick Diderot taught us in JACQUES LE FATALISTE.

Raymond Federman

Where? -- Where? Reader you are of a rather cumbersome curiosity!
By the devil what does it matter? Even if I were to tell you that it was
in Pontoise or in Saint-Germain, or in Notre-Dame de Lorette or
Saint-Jacques de Compostelle, would you be better off? But if you
insist, I will tell you that they were going toward -- yes, why not? -- an
immense castle, on the frontispiece of which was written: I belong to
no one and I belong to everyone. You were here already before
entering, and you will still be here after departing.

What a shrewd way of getting around the problem. Diderot really
understood that to get on with the story one must avoid precision. One
must digress. Skip around. Improvise. Leave blank what cannot be
filled in. Offer multiple choices. Deviate from the facts, from the
where and the when, in order to reach the truth. Why this obstinate
need to give stories a neat beginning, middle, and end?

The grim story of Sarah and her cousin should be told without any
mention of time and place. It should happen on a timeless vacant stage
without scenery. No names of places. No decor. Nothing. It simply
happened, sometime and somewhere. And one day, totally lost, the
two cousins can wonder if they are part of the world, or if the world is
simply they thinking that there is such a place. How much easier, and

how much more profound it becomes when one skips the specificity of time and place.

Once upon a time, after the war, the cousin went away to one place, and Sarah to another. They were separated for many years. Doesn't matter how long, or which war. All wars separate people. All wars make orphans of children and mourners of parents. They suffered. Years later, when they were reunited, they cried.

That's how it should be told, with total disregard for precision. The two cousins simply stranded on the threshold of their adventure so that they can never look back on what happened. The beginning of their story cancelling everything in advance. But since they belong to a race doomed to survival by its impatience and inability to remain still, they have to be put in motion so that eventually they can confront themselves. Even a beginning that cancels itself is the beginning of something. Ah, but to start the way Diderot does, with boldness and effrontery.

How did they meet? By chance like everyone else. What were their names? What do you care? Where were they coming from? The nearest place. Where were they going? Does one really know where one is going? What where they saying? The master was not saying anything, but Jacques was saying that his captain was saying that everything that happens to us here on earth, good or bad, is written above.

So much already at work in this beginning. The sense of rhythm, the quick tempo of those initial sentences in the form of questions and answers that annul each other. And of course, the irrealism of it. I know of no opening more fascinating, more engaging than this one.

Hey! maybe I could call the cousin Jacques? In honor of Diderot. Not a bad choice. Cousin Jacques the Optimist. Jacques the Stone Carver! ... No. No Sarah's cousin should remain unnamed. I know, you're going to tell me I'm wasting my time playing these games just because I don't know how to begin this story. You're right. I should not fool around like this simply because I refuse to submit to the paralyzing holiness of realism.

Well let me assure you, I would gladly sacrifice all the tricks and gimmicks that have sustained me so far if I could rid myself of the imposture of realism, that ugly beast that stands at bay ready to leap in the moment you begin scribbling your fiction. Sarah's story should not be touched by the banality of realism. It's too fragile. Reality is a form of disenchantment. The only reason it interests us is because behind it always lurks a catastrophe, or a bad joke.

Here, let me show you. On the very spot where Aunt Basha's apartment building once stood, the exact spot where the old aunt abandoned Sarah to rush to her cowardly survival, now stands a museum. I'm not kidding. On that very spot. A museum of modern art. A gigantic structure made of glass and steel, painted bright blue and green. A monstrosity. What a fabulous piece of erasure! What a scandalous substitution! The immorality of history replaced by the playfulness of modern art. The old shabby building transformed into a comic book scenery, and all is well again so that the fable can go on in the hysteria of urban renewal. They call that face-lifting, but it's really an efface-ment. That's how the imposture of realism works, by erasure and substitution.

When the nine year old Sarah stood in front of Basha's building and watched her aunt take off in her fur coat with her suitcase full of riches, little did she know that someday, on that very spot, a mausoleum to art would proclaim victory over the fiasco of history -- her history! One must refuse such cringing ironies. That is why it is essential to avoid the specificity of time and place, even at the risk of skirting allegory.

Raymond Federman

History is a joke whose punch line is always messed up in advance. But
since this is not the story of what happened, and how it was or was not
resolved, but of the consequences of what happened, there is no need
of a punch line.

What the cousins are seeking is not the meaning of what happened, but
the meaning of an absence. The absence of pain. Their bodies bear
no inscriptions of suffering since they escaped physical pain, hunger,
and torture. In a way they suffered from not suffering enough. The
suffering of Sarah and her cousin was never adequate, it dissipated into
the incomprehension of suffering. That is why the void of their lives
can only find its fulfillment in the circumstances of that void. It is not
the pain of an instant, the suffering of a single moment that matters. It
is the remembrance one cultivates for a lifetime. For the cousins that
remembrance is of an absence, and they have made a lifetime occasion
of it.

But enough of that. Instead let's go see what the cousin is doing. By
now he must have dozed off in the waiting lounge, the unread book still
open on his lap. No. Rather, let's go find Sarah and Elie at the other
airport, and leave the cousin to his erotic fantasies.

To Whom It May Concern

Sarah! I'm not going to cry when I see him. She doesn't say that, her body says it. I'm not going to cry. It is as if Sarah's whole being braces itself for this refusal of emotion, this denial of tears. He may not even recognize her, not even remember how she looks ... Will she recognize him when he steps off the plane? He must have changed too in thirty-five years. He was so handsome, looked so much like his father with his wavy hair and impetuous eyes. Those photographs they exchanged over the years were they really them? How old is he now? He was eighteen when he left. Sarah suddenly remembers what her cousin said on the platform of the train station as he set out into his exile. I must go, I must go find a future. The corners of her mouth turn into a smile. Those words sound so ponderous now, so melodramatic.

While Elie is reading his newspaper Sarah wanders into the past, back to the moment when she and her cousin found each other at the end of the war, and learned that their parents, brothers and sisters had been destroyed. She remembers how difficult it was for them to manage. She revisits the little corner they had set up as a home in the basement of a demolished building. Everything above that cellar was in ruins. Bombed out. For nearly two years, the cousins lived in that hole, like gypsies, until they were forced to move when the city decided to clear away the ruins. They had furnished it with objects they found in the buildings crushed by air raids. A table with three legs that had to be

109

propped against the wall to stand, two wobbly chairs, a torn mattress. Sarah remembers how the two of them lay awake on that mattress close to each other, looking at the sky through a small gap in the cellar's ceiling, a gap the shape of a fish, and how night after night they tried to tell each other what happened after their parents were taken away, and they found themselves abandoned -- Sarah in the street, her cousin in a closet.

Sarah would start talking, in a whisper as if afraid to let the words escape, but then she would stop and stare into the darkness, and her cousin would ask, what's wrong? She would not answer, but he knew what was wrong, as she did too when he stopped in the middle of his story. Nothing was really wrong, just that the story refused to be spoken.

Then they separated. Though they wrote each other regularly, at least during the first years, they never again mentioned what had happened. It was as if a moment of their lives had been blurred, had been deleted. But perhaps there was purpose, even satisfaction in their inability to speak that moment.

To Whom It May Concern

Elie folds his newspaper. I'm going to see if there is any news of his flight. I'll be back in a minute. Do you want me to bring you something to drink?

Sarah shakes her head, no thanks. She stands up to stretch. She suddenly feels uncomfortable. Why did she have to put on this silly dress? She's more herself, more like herself in pants. She never wears dresses. Except for special occasions. When her daughter got married. For the funeral of Elie's brother. What a sad day that was. His younger brother killed in one of those stupid attacks. She feels so clumsy in this sleeveless blue dress with its starchy white collar. And why is she carrying this purse? The thin fabric of the dress clings to her body in the heat. She feels as if her hips, her breasts, are exposed. Why did she have to ask Elie if she should wear a dress to go to the airport? A dress might be more appropriate, Elie said. Gentle Elie, so considerate. Why more appropriate? Suddenly Sarah is angry with herself, angry for being the prey of restless and foolish impulses. She wonders if her cousin will be embarrassed when he sees what she is, what she has become. Will they have anything to say to each other?

Elie returns. Nothing new. They say his plane will probably arrive at eight o'clock, but that's not confirmed.

It's only five-thirty now, what do we do? I hate waiting in airports. It's so boring.

What else can we do? Elie shrugs his shoulders. There is no point going into the city. It's a good forty-five minutes away. What will we do there? And anyway the city must be full of soldiers and policemen searching for the terrorists. We've waited here this long, what's another two or three hours. Look, why don't we get a cup of coffee or something.

They walk to the terrace of the airport café. The place is buzzing. Everyone is still talking about the bombing. It seems that one of the terrorists was caught, but two others have escaped. Sarah's hand shakes a little as she lifts her cup. Elie, maybe we should try to call Yossi, she says, maybe Yossi can ...

What can Yossi do about the plane? You always think Yossi can solve everything.

No, I don't mean about the plane, but about the bombing. I'm ... I'm worried.

To Whom It May Concern

Look, it's his job. And how do you know he's involved?

I know. I know he's involved. Yossi is always involved.

They are silent for a while. A huge plane glides overhead toward the runway. Everybody looks up. They're letting planes land again, Sarah says. Maybe his will arrive sooner than they said. Then she adds as if thinking aloud, I still can't believe he's coming. Me too, Elie says. I'm really curious to meet him. And it'll be interesting to see what kind of work he does.

They are making small talk, repeating all they have said before, just to pass the time.

Isn't that something Elie, my cousin a famous artist! A sculptor! But I shouldn't be surprised. When he was young there was something about him, something mysterious about his quiet stubbornness and moodiness. I remember how he would sit for hours just staring into nothing.

Raymond Federman

I suppose he is famous, otherwise the museum wouldn't have invited him. But isn't it strange that he never talked about his work in his letters. Not a word. Never sent a catalogue. Nothing.

That's true. But you know, it's not that unusual, a lot of artists don't like to talk about their work. Maybe he's like that. Though he did send us an article once, about him. Don't you remember? It appeared in a glossy magazine.

Oh yes I remember now. It was like an interview with him about the way he works. There was even a photograph of him with the article. Wasn't there? But that was a long time ago. At least fifteen years, maybe more.

That's right, a picture of him in his studio standing next to one of his sculptures. I must still have that picture.

Yes, a huge piece of sculpture. He looked so small next to it. It was hard to tell what it was supposed to represent. It seemed to be made of metal and plastic twisted together. I remember we thought it looked violent.

To Whom It May Concern

You're right. In fact, the article mentioned how strange and violent his work is. It said that the reason his sculptures are so unusual is because he uses all sorts of different material besides metal or stone. Things like plastic, cloth, leather, even bones, bones from dead animals, and that's what makes his work appear so savage and violent. You know, I'm not sure I'm going to like it. When it comes to art I like pleasant things, and I like to be able to recognize what I'm looking at.

Sarah becomes thoughtful. She just remembered what her cousin said in the article when he was asked if he used bones in his sculptures to suggest death. His answer struck her at the time. If the wood in my work hesitates to be a tree, or the leather to be skin, why should the bones be death. Bone is just a material like any other. What a strange answer. It's as though he was denying the meaning of his work. As though he was afraid of its implications. But maybe it was just a period. The violence. Artists have different periods in their work. Who knows, what he does now may be quite different. More gentle and meaningful. As one gets older ...

You know, it's hard to judge from only one picture in a magazine, Sarah says emerging from her thoughts. I suppose we'll have a chance to see for ourselves.

Raymond Federman

Elie doesn't answer. He unfolds his newspaper and begins to read again. Sarah retreats into herself and wonders if her cousin has changed much. He was so gentle, so caring with her. Though always stubborn and determined with everything else. Has he become angry? Does he see only the dark side of life?

Why he is coming alone, without his wife and daughter? The way he talks about them in his letters, he must love them very much, be very close to them. He did say in his last letter that they might join him later. Perhaps because of the show and all the publicity he prefers to be alone at first. Still why wouldn't he want them to share that with him? Sarah has often tried to imagine what sort of a woman his wife is. Her cousin never said much about her, except he did write soon after they were married that she too had had a difficult experience during the war. Sarah would like so much to know her. And his daughter too. She must be about the same age as Yossi. He speaks of her with such tenderness. How can a man who shows such love for his daughter be so violent in his work?

Will he be cold and distant? Disinterested? Sarah's mind is racing from one thought to another. Does he still remember what she used to write when she first arrived here? Her letters seemed to annoy him

116

because she kept insisting that he should move here, that he belonged here. And he would reply, I know, you're right, I belong there. Be patient, you'll see I'll come soon. But he never did.

Though he kept writing to Sarah that things were going well, the first years of his exile were a total disenchantment as he stumbled from one misfortune to another. From one failure to another. His life had no direction, no purpose. Yet he kept finding more reasons and excuses for not being able to join Sarah. He led a solitary and self-centered life, doing odd jobs just to keep going. But one day he discovered in his hands the meaning of his life.

He was alone in a restaurant waiting for his meal to be served when he found himself absentmindedly shaping a human figure with the soft center of a piece of bread. It was a clumsy figure, but it felt familiar to his hands. His fingers were molding the face, his thumbs pressing in where the eyes would be, when suddenly he stopped as he felt an unexpected exhilaration. This form without substance, this being without life was trying to tell him something. He got up and left the restaurant without waiting for his food. He walked a long time in the streets his head bowed, lost in thoughts. The next few days he went from museum to museum to look at sculptures. He spent hours in front of the same statue trying to understand what it was, and how it had been made. Sometimes he would approach the stone and touch it. He would let his hand rest on a curve or feel a slit in the stone until the museum guard would tell him not to touch the artwork. Slowly he began to realize that in the space a statue occupies it gives form to an absence. His whole life he had been obsessed with absence, and now he had found a way to render that absence present. He devoted the next few years to the study of art. Forced to work during the day he went to school in the evening. He became obsessed with his studies and read everything he could find about the masters. Eventually his work as a sculptor took over his entire existence. Everything else became secondary.

Now, waiting for her cousin to arrive, Sarah wonders if he's still angry because she urged him so often to come. She shakes her head, as if answering her own question. No, that was so long ago.

After he left, Sarah lived with a young couple she and her cousin had met at a gathering of people whose families disappeared during the war. Not much older than the cousins, they too had managed to survive. Marco and Olga met in deportation, helped each other endure pain and hunger, fell in love, and now married with a one year old child, they

were learning to adjust to their survival. Sarah and her cousin often
spent evenings with Marco and Olga sharing their food, and talking
about the future. When Sarah was denied a visa to go with her cousin,
because of the tuberculous spot on her lung, she insisted that he go
alone. Marco and Olga offered to take care of her until she was cured
and could join him. Sarah moved in with them. They put a folding cot
for her in the kitchen. She didn't mind. They were kind. They treated
her like a little sister, and she was happy with them. She cared for the
baby while Marco and Olga went to work. Marco had found a job with
a tailor who was teaching him how to make men's pants. Olga worked
as a seamstress in a small dress shop.

Her cousin left a little money for Sarah's care, money he had saved
working in a factory, and he promised to send more every month so
that Sarah could get treatments for her tuberculosis.

Alone all day with the baby, Sarah spent her time playing mother. She
liked that, though sometimes it made her sad because she too felt the
need of a mother's care. Fifteen but still a child, she was too old now
to go back to school. For the rest of her life she would have to resign
herself to this gap of ignorance and this lack of motherly affection.
Often she took the child to the nearby park. Sometimes she would even

roll the baby carriage all the way to her old neighborhood and for hours she would wander in the streets as if searching for something, as if expecting her parents and brothers to appear suddenly in front of her. Even six years after they were taken away she still fantasized it would happen, just like that.

One day in the park a girl about the same age came and sat beside her on the bench. She too was taking care of a baby. Her name was Iris. She had a round face with quick eyes, short hair, and hands that gesticulated all the time when she spoke. Her parents too had disappeared in the war, and like Sarah she suffered of loneliness and absence. The two girls talked for a long time, at first about the babies and the parents of the babies, but then gradually they told each other the story of how each had managed to escape.

Sarah told Iris how her mother had sent her to get a loaf of bread when the soldiers came to arrest them and how the woman who lived next door wanted to take her to the police so she could be put with her parents and how she ran away from this woman and wandered all day waiting for her family to come home and later that afternoon she saw her Aunt Basha leave in a taxi but the aunt didn't talk to her she just waved from inside the taxi and left Sarah behind all alone and after that she walked in the streets some more until this girl Josette who was a prostitute took care of her. Sarah told her story quickly, almost in a whisper.

Then Iris told how she fell off a train. A freight car full of children. She didn't know where the train was going. This was after she was separated from her parents. She fell while the train was moving fast. Iris laughed, an embarrassed giggle, when she told Sarah how it happened. The freight car was packed with all these children who were crying and screaming. It was very hot in the train. A boy tried to force the door open to let in some air. Iris was squeezed against it and when it jerked open she fell. Maybe somebody pushed her by accident. She fell into a ditch and stayed there a long time until an old farmer found her. She was moaning because her leg was broken. The farmer took her to his house and a doctor came to set the leg. He put a huge cast on her. She was nine when that happened. The farmer and his wife said it was a miracle the way she fell off the train and survived. They went around telling the other farmers that she had fallen from the sky. The old farmers were nice to her, and she helped around the farm, but one night the farmer's wife died and after the funeral the old man took Iris in his horse carriage to a convent. She stayed there until the end of the war, but she was very unhappy. The nuns made her pray and work hard all the time.

Sarah and her new friend met again, almost every day. Iris was the only person to whom Sarah could talk without holding back or feeling ashamed. Even to her cousin she could not tell all that happened. Unlike Sarah who lived her misfortunes passively and seemed not to be aware of what was going on around her, Iris was full of life and full of awareness. She told Sarah about this group of young people, survivors like them who were preparing to go to a place far away that needed people who could dedicate themselves to building a new country. It's just a piece of desert right now, Iris explained, but with hard work it can become a beautiful place. A home. A real home for us. A few months after her cousin went away, Sarah and her new friend joined this group and left for the desert. Sarah didn't even write to her cousin to ask for his advice. She just went.

That was thirty-five years ago. Sarah's eyes suddenly blur as she remembers how, only a few weeks after they arrived at the camp farm on the border, Iris was shot in the chest during one of the night raids. Two days later she died holding Sarah's hand.

Sarah fumbles in her purse for a handkerchief. She blows her nose and wipes her eyes. Elie looks up from his newspaper. Don't tell me you're catching a cold in this heat. No, I just got something in my eye, Sarah answers turning her face away. She shakes her head to rid her mind of that sad memory. Suddenly a twisted smile forms at the corner of her mouth as she remembers what her Aunt Basha said when she told her she was leaving. That's a good idea, the old aunt said approvingly. Yes, it's a good place over there for orphans like you.

Soon after the war Aunt Basha returned to the city. She was the only other member of the entire family to return. All the others had disappeared, even her own husband and her two sons, but somehow the old aunt managed to stay alive. She moved back into her old apartment and lived there alone with her things, rarely going out, until she died of old age. Eventually Aunt Basha's building was demolished and a museum of modern art was built on that very spot.

One day Sarah and her cousin saw their aunt in the street. They had no idea she was back. This was just a few weeks after they found each other at the end of the war. At first the children were not sure it was Aunt Basha. She looked old, very old, her hair gray now, her face wrinkled, and she walked hunched over. But it was their aunt. They rushed to her shouting her name. She didn't seem to recognize them, and when they came close she brushed them aside. She went on walking, dragging one leg, while talking to herself aloud. Sarah and her

cousin walked along with her and tried to explain who they were. She
kept shaking her head and saying, no no go away, but then she asked
them to carry the bag of food she was holding in her arms like a baby.
They carried it up the dark stairs to her apartment on the fifth floor,
the same apartment the children had visited so often in the past. The
place was dark, dusty and musty, with broken objects strewn all over
the floor. Some of the furniture was covered with dirty sheets. The
windows were shut, and the window-panes streaked. Sarah and her
cousin became scared of this woman who acted like a stranger, yet they
needed to tell her that they were the children of her sister and brother
who were taken away, but Basha kept pushing them away and shaking
her head as if she didn't want to hear what they were saying. Then she
started screaming while wringing her hands in front of her face. She
pushed the children toward the door, and shouted, go now go, but then
she changed her mind, no wait a minute, she said lowering her voice,
and she stared at them as if trying to remember something.

When Sarah and her cousin finally left, they ran all the way down the
dark stairwell and away from Basha's building holding hands. They
never went back to that apartment, though once in a while they would
see their aunt walking in the street talking to herself, and always
carrying a bag of food. They would avoid her. But one time, when
Sarah was alone, she saw her aunt coming out of a store, and she

approached her to try again to tell her who she was, but when she came close she saw how Basha's face had become all yellow like a mask, and how the eyes were full of pus. It was so scary, Sarah rushed away without talking to her. Yet when she decided to leave for the desert with Iris, Sarah went and told her old aunt, and that's when Basha said, yes it's a good idea, it's a good place for orphans like you.

Orphans! Sarah wonders if she is still an orphan. And her cousin too. Does he still think of himself as an orphan? Does one still think oneself an orphan when one gets older? Past fifty? Does one continue to be an orphan when one becomes older than one's parents? Older than they were when they died? Sarah's mother was thirty-two, her father thirty-four when they were taken away to be destroyed. At which moment in one's life does one cease to be an orphan?

Sitting next to Elie at the terrace of the café in the heat of the afternoon, Sarah closes her eyes and sinks deeper into herself. On the stage of her mind she sees a little girl standing in front of the building where she lived, looking up at the windows of the apartment on the third floor. One of her hands is shading her eyes from the sun. It's a beautiful day in May. The war is over. The streets are crowded with people. When finally Sarah turns away from the building she sees her cousin standing across the street. Frozen in place. They stare at one another as if trying to remember who they are. And then as they move hesitantly toward each other, he cries out, Sarah, it's you, it's you! And she too cries out, it's you! And now they rush toward one another and embrace, right there in the middle of the crowded street. Then after the tears, and the hugs, and the stroking of each other's faces, he asks, are your parents and sisters back? And she says, no. And he says, nor are mine.

Later that night, in the cellar of the demolished building, the two cousins huddled on the bare mattress, and there, among the ruins, tried to learn who they were, who they had become, now that they had emerged from the great tumult. That night, as they lay awake next to each other looking at the sky through the hole in the ceiling, Sarah said with great urgency in her voice, teach me to be strong. Teach me. I need to be strong. Her cousin did not answer, but he reached for her face and placed his hand on her mouth.

Night after night they would repeat the same words, ask the same questions, and wonder if they would ever again see their families. Sarah would ask, do you think they'll come back soon?

To Whom It May Concern

Your parents and mine? Your brothers, and my sisters? Everybody?
I don't know. I really don't know. Since I got back three weeks ago,
I've been asking around. I even inquired at the Ministry of the Victims
of the War. They don't know anything. Some people are coming back.
Not many. Nobody seems to know what happened to all the others.

Night after night, in the hole of that cellar, Sarah and her cousin
whispered to each other fragments of their story. But they could never
go on with it. You tell me first, she would say. No you first, her cousin
would insist. You tell me where you were and how you managed all
alone. And so Sarah would begin, but she would soon stop and ask,
always with the same anguish in her voice, why did they do that?

And her cousin would answer, I don't know, I don't know. That's the
way people are. Sometimes people do things like that to each other for
no reason.

But we didn't do anything wrong, Sarah would say with indignant tears
forming at the corners of her eyes.

That's the way people are ...

Raymond Federman

Oh no, that's too easy to say. But then it will take many years for Sarah and her cousin to understand that the enormity which consumed their parents, brothers and sisters, had little to do with the way people are. People are dragged into history in spite of themselves. What happened was just an inescapable fact of history, and Sarah and her cousin will have to learn that ultimately everything fades into banality -- horror as well as fear.

You must be wondering how I can go on circling around Sarah and her cousin without being able to grasp their story. Listen, do we not always speak well and abundantly of the great deeds we would like to accomplish, but when the time comes to perform these deeds we seem incapable of doing so. Most of our life is spent in the if of our desires and regrets, and I am as iffy as the next guy, always slipping into further abandonment. But who knows, this conditional incapacity is perhaps destined to have its place in the work process, assigned to it by a furor devoid of desires and regrets. So bear with me. Perhaps soon I'll give you the whole story.

To Whom It May Concern

Monday, February 6

It's been over a month since I last spoke of Sarah. I thought I had lost her story, but it had only faded into some remote corner of my mind. This morning Sarah is back, asking to be spoken. Meanwhile not a word from you either this past month. A most unusual silence. I am worried, particularly since, the last time, you spoke of the leap, the great leap you were intending. I did not understand, and then I read in the newspaper about Primo Levi hurling himself to his death down some stairwell, and me, informed mostly by my own present blackness of spirit, I imagined your substantial abyss of darkness and thought that … in an insane moment, or even something like joy, you would yourself … but I resisted that notion.

129

Raymond Federman

Write quick to say the leap of which you spoke was only a metaphor. On a clear cold day like today one should not entertain such morbid thoughts but seek the restoration of the original happiness. But then, I wonder, how does one measure the distance between the original happiness and the final panic? Perhaps there is no distance between the two. It is possible to believe that on a clear cold day like today, one lazy afternoon a long time ago, with nothing better to do, some happy fellow invented death by jumping off a cliff.

You see what a month of silence does to me. Quickly then, let me speak of Sarah. Let me speak of survival rather than death.

It was dark when Josette returned to the purple room where Sarah was still asleep. A dark, hot, and humid night. The sky had turned stormy with threatening gray clouds as if the weather had decided to play its part in the ugly drama of that day. I am, of course, imagining this. For all I know the sky may have been clear and indifferent.

The city was getting more and more frantic in the presence of the round-up. Trucks full of people were racing toward the collecting centers and dispatching stations. Policemen, soldiers, militiamen were everywhere, searching buildings, guarding train stations and bus terminals, stopping cars and buses at the roadblocks that had been set up at all roads leading out of the city. The clean-up operation, at it was called, had reached a peak of frenzy and desperation. People who tried to escape by hiding in basements, attics, closets, or the sewers of the city were being uncovered and brutally hauled to the trucks. Everywhere tears were protesting the insolence of the moment.

A soldier searching the basement of a building found a woman hiding inside a cardboard box. She was crying quietly while holding a dead little girl in her arms, an apple stuck in the child's mouth. A boy forgotten in a corridor ran into the street between two soldiers who were chasing a man. The soldiers fired and a bullet struck the boy in the back of the head. He fell forward. The man stopped. He knelt next to the body and placed his hand on the boy's exploded head. The blood trickled through his fingers. He then faced the soldiers standing a few feet away, their rifles still pointing, and stared at them. Suddenly his freedom, his life became irrelevant. Slowly the man rose and walked toward the soldiers. When he reached them, he grabbed one of the rifles, put the muzzle in his mouth and fired. Without hesitation, without rehearsal, this man had reached instantly for the great disembodied wisdom.

Raymond Federman

By evening, neighbors who were afraid to be implicated pointed out the places where people were hiding. It was as if the whole city now wanted to get this thing over with as quickly as possible and deny what ought not to be, as if the good citizens of the Republic wanted to make certain that no evidence would outlive them.

The soldiers and policemen were getting more and more anxious and violent, pushing people down staircases, kicking them, striking them with their weapons. The somewhat apologetic attitude of the early morning had turned brutal and vicious. But then brutality and viciousness are always the disguises of those who want to abolish conscience.

All afternoon, after she locked Sarah in her room, Josette rushed from one official building to another trying to find out what had happened to Sarah's family. Since she didn't want to give the reason for her inquiry, she made up a story about the cat that had been left behind in the apartment next to hers. She explained that she was a neighbor and she could hear the cat meowing desperately inside the empty apartment. She kept smiling and being flirtatious with the men she spoke to. Most of them were indifferent to her questions, but not to her charms. Josette soon discovered that everything was confusion, and

To Whom It May Concern

that no one really knew much about this whole affair. Finally she gave
up. She became fearful that she too might be arrested even though she
kept flashing her papers to prove that she was not one of those people
who carried special identification cards in addition to the patch on their
clothing. She lost her composure and became frightened when an
officer at one of the headquarters found her cat story unlikely and her
interest in these people very suspicious. He wanted to know if she was
related to them. Josette insisted she was not, that she was only concerned about the cat because if it stayed in that apartment without food
it might die, and there was no way to get in without the keys. The
elegant young officer walked around his desk and stood in front of
Josette looking straight into her face. Josette panicked and tears
started to form in her eyes, but she managed to take hold of herself and
somehow eased her way out of his suspicions with smiles, and by letting
him touch her body. After that she rushed home.

Now Josette was standing in her room watching Sarah sleep. She had
not turned on the light when she came in, but the glare of a street lamp
reached into the room. She stood there for a while contemplating
Sarah's face, listening to her soft breathing. There is such purity in the
face of a sleeping child. The doll had rolled out of Sarah's arms and
was lying face down next to her, its laced panties exposed under the
red dress. Josette leaned over Sarah and turned the doll on its back.

Why was she so concerned about this little girl? Was it the surge of responsibility one feels in the encounter with the face of another human being, especially that of a child, that had made her act so spontaneously? But what was she going to do now with this little girl? She couldn't keep her. Where could she take her? She didn't know anybody, and none of the other girls in the street had volunteered to help. They quickly disappeared after Josette took Sarah up the stairs. Where would she hide her when she brought the men up to her room? In her closet? Under the bed with the chamber pot? Why did she have to get involved with this thing? She had no particular feeling about what was going on that day in the city. It had nothing to do with her. Sure she felt sorry for all these people being herded away, but she had her own problems, her own private misery to attend to. The circumstances of the moment had forced her to become what she was, and she even let enemy soldiers make love to her. She was ashamed of that, and yet, right now, it was the only way to survive. She had nothing, nothing else to sell.

Her father had been killed in the war just before the final defeat. Josette was fifteen then. Her mother became ill, and eventually was sent to a mental institution. The doctor explained to Josette that her mother's mind had faded away. Once a month Josette visited her mother. She sat next to her, next to this woman who talked aloud to herself, drooled, and who did not even recognize her own daughter. But Josette had no one else. No other family. After her mother was sent away, she moved in with neighbors. Pauline, a friend of her mother, felt sorry for her and took her in. She was kind and tried to help Josette get over the pain, but Pauline had her own problems with her three small children, and especially with her husband, an angry brutal factory worker who often came home drunk. In the small crowded apartment, especially now with an extra person, he often teased and fondled the young girl even in front of Pauline. The situation became unbearable for Josette. The children yelling and crying all the time. Pauline losing her temper and hitting them. The ugly hands of the husband constantly reaching for her. He had tattoos on top of both hands. An anchor on the left one, and a heart pierced by an arrow on the right one. Josette was frightened by this annexation of her body ...

Well well, how do you like that! Here I am suddenly in the middle of a good old-fashioned melodrama. This is starting to sound like Nana. Pure solid naturalism. I really had no intention of getting that involved with Josette's sordid existence, but once a prostitute walks into your book inevitably all kinds of sad familiar tales come bursting upon you. You see, most people live in a common unrecorded place, protected from the horrors of history. Others, like Sarah and her cousin, and

Josette too, have had to live in history. That is why the details of their story are of little consequence, but not their passage in history. And yet, it is always the story, the story with its details that demands to be told. But isn't it true that to tell a story is to discredit it? I mean, to tell it unfractured from the cozy realm of conventional practices. Josette's story also deserves to be told. She played an important role in Sarah's survival, and as a result was hurled into history. It's a problem though, because if this book is to gain integrity, it will be from the denial of anecdotes. That is the central doctrine here. But what worries me is that if I persist in this refusal of details, the whole enterprise might crumble into vagueness and obscurity, and that might go against the necessity of what must be told.

Why worry about that now. This is not the final resting place of this book. What has been told so far is only temporary. I'm just trying out things. Later I can always delete the naturalistic stuff. But no need to go on with Josette's life. You can imagine the rest yourself. You know, the usual sentimental story of how a young girl becomes a prostitute, with the same hope of redemption at the end. Yes, no need to go on with that. Instead let's return to what happened to Sarah and her cousin on that bleak day.

To Whom It May Concern

While Josette watched Sarah sleep it didn't occur to her that perhaps she had seen this girl before. Yes, possibly she had noticed her when, on their way to visit Aunt Basha, Sarah's brothers had dragged their little sister past the spot where Josette usually stood. She could not have anticipated then that one day her fate would become entangled with hers. And when Josette asked Sarah why she was crying, she did not realize that in asking that question she gave purpose to her own life. Now Josette had to assume the consequences of her curiosity.

Sarah stirred on the bed, unfolded her legs and sighed. Josette went to the window to shut the curtains, and then she turned on the light. Sarah blinked and rubbed the sleep from her eyes with the back of her hands. Josette sat on the edge of the bed and gently ran her fingers through the child's hair. She said nothing, and Sarah didn't ask if she found her parents. She just let Josette's hand play with her hair. Sleep had carried her to the other side of her adventure. Already the events of the day were blocked in her mind. For a long time the two of them remained silent, oblivious to the before and the after of this moment. Sarah unaware that she was fatally sliding toward abandonment, and Josette trying to postpone the inevitable decision of what to do with this child. They were learning to be with each other, at least for now, without any sense of what lay ahead of them. There was no logic to their being here together, as there would be no logic to what would

Raymond Federman

happen afterwards. The present is always unvarnished. Only the past and the future are in the domain of ambiguity. Outside the room, where Josette and Sarah waited suspended in time, the trucks and the trains continued to roll into the night.

Meanwhile, in another part of the city, that same day, at the same hour, Sarah's cousin, twelve years old, was sitting half- naked on a pile of old newspapers inside a closet. He had been there since early that morning. As the soldiers came up the stairs to take his parents and sisters away, and him too, his mother awoke him. It was five in the morning. The soldiers were already calling their names as they made their way up the stairs, and his mother pushed him into the little closet on the landing of the staircase. She didn't say anything, she just put a finger over her mouth to show him to be quiet, and closed the door. His eyes were still full of sleep, and he only had on the shorts he slept with. From behind the door of the closet he heard his name called by the soldiers, and he heard his father say something but too softly to understand what it was, and then he heard the steps of his mother and father and sisters, and those of the soldiers too, going down the stairs, and he heard doors opening and closing, and voices in the staircase, and then all was quiet. He sat in the closet, darkness in his eyes, dust in his mouth, afraid to come out because the people who lived downstairs might see him and tell, but also embarrassed because he only wore his underwear.

138

To Whom It May Concern

He stayed all day in that closet, on the top floor of the building. It was dark inside, and hot. He didn't dare open the door. He kept hearing people coming up to the door of his apartment, just outside his closet. Then he heard that door being forced open, and he heard the noise the people made inside the apartment as they moved things around. Trembling with fear and incomprehension, the boy did not understand that the people in the building were already plundering his home. But somehow in their haste they ignored the closet where he was hiding.

Hours later, when the building was quiet again, the boy groped in the dark along the walls of the closet. Behind the newspapers he found an old pair of shoes and a box full of sugar cubes. High on the wall he felt a coat hanging from a nail, and on a shelf above the coat a hat. He recognized his father's winter overcoat and hat. He felt guilty when he searched inside the pockets of his father's coat. He found a key, a safety pin, a pencil stub, a coin, and some loose tobacco. He took the coat down, folded it and placed it next to him on the pile of newspapers. Then he tried on the shoes. They were too big. He ate some of the sugar, letting the cubes melt in his mouth. Though he was a little scared of the dark, being in that closet was like a game, except that he didn't know when he was supposed to stop playing. Or maybe it was a punishment. His mother put him in here because he had done something wrong, and he had to stay until she came back and said he could come out.

Later in the afternoon, he needed to shit, but he didn't know what to do. He tried to hold back as long as he could, but finally twisting with pain he unfolded a newspaper, crouched over it and defecated, holding his penis away from his legs so as not to wet himself. He used a piece of the newspaper to wipe himself. As he wrapped the paper into a neat package, he felt the wetness and the warmth on his hands. He placed the package on the floor near the door and smelled his hands. Later when he finally dared open the door, it was night outside. Rays of moonlight filtered down from the skylight at the top of the staircase just above his closet. His face squeezed in the narrow opening of the door, he listened for a while. He heard voices behind doors downstairs. They were soft, he couldn't tell what they were saying. He held his parcel in one hand away from his face and tiptoed up to the skylight. He pushed the glass open a little, squeezed the parcel in the opening and placed it on the roof. He tiptoed back down into his closet and waited, sitting on the newspapers. Once in a while he would go to the door, open it just a crack and listen. The people downstairs were still talking. He waited some more. He took some sugar cubes out of the box and sucked on them. Before closing the box he put a handful of cubes in the pocket of his father's coat, for later.

To Whom It May Concern

Late in the night he finally put on his father's coat and hat. The coat reached to his ankles, the hat drooped over his eyes. He slipped his bare feet inside the shoes. The heels clattered as he stepped to the door. He took the shoes off and held them in his hands. A small parody of his father, he emerged on the landing. It got darker and darker as he went down the stairs. Some of the steps were creaking. He tried to take two at a time but he stepped on the coat, stumbled and fell. He let go of the shoes and they rolled down the stairs with a frightening noise. He got back on his feet, and holding the coat up as a woman would her skirts he ran the rest of the way down. Just as he reached the ground floor he heard a door open above and a man shout, who is there? He stood frozen in place for a moment, not daring to look back for fear of being transfigured. Finally he ran out into the street, barefoot.

Over the years, Sarah's cousin often reentered that closet and there tried to decipher in the blackness of that hole the meaning of his mother's gesture. Now, the day he is to be reunited with Sarah, stranded in the city where it happened long ago, once again he will relive that moment, and enter that closet. There he will watch the boy sitting on a pile of newspapers, knees folded to his chin, and again he will feel the fear of darkness and abandonment. Standing on the landing outside the closet, he will see the boy's head emerge in the

Raymond Federman

narrow opening of the door, and he will follow him up the stairs to the
skylight carrying his package of excrement, and again he will feel on
his hands the intolerable warmth and wetness of this filthy parcel, and
after the boy has placed it on the roof to disintegrate in the wind, he
will follow him down the stairs and watch him vanish into the night,
clown-like in his father's coat and hat.

Eyes half-closed as if dozing, there at the airport, the cousin will
wonder what to call the day he was left in the closet. What to call that
terrible moment? Or was it a fortunate occasion? Should he call it a
birth? A salvation? Or should he name it the beginning of a long
absence from himself? Suddenly, on the day of reunion, he will recognize himself as a mythical being. An Orpheus. But not the Orpheus
who sang love songs in the tunnel of death. An Orpheus who carved
his way out of the stone block into which he was buried alive. Yes this
time, as he follows the boy down the stairs, he will understand that if
he stops, turns to look back, something unspeakable will happen. His
own death will be unmasked as a false resurrection.

On the day when he and Sarah will embrace again, he will realize that
he spent his entire life fearing the light shining through human skin, but
he will also realize that death is not something you solve, death is

142

something you enter, as you do a closet. Perhaps the foetus that he was in that closet should have been left there throbbing in the dark forever so it could by-pass mortality. Or else, like the parcel of excrement on the roof, it should have been allowed to disintegrate in the wind. And yet this foetus had to come out of that closet-tomb, otherwise it would never have learned the strength that comes from despair and the ingenuity that arises from necessity. This he will have to explain to Sarah when she asks, with the same urgency as when she was a child, how he managed to go on all these years.

There is so much he will have to tell her. This time the gap, the distance between them will have to be spanned. This time they will have to tell each other everything once and for all. And so waiting for his plane to depart, he begins to rehearse what he will tell Sarah when she asks: and then after the boy ran into the street, what happened? Just as he will ask her: and you, after Josette returned, what happened? You tell me first, Sarah will say. And he will. But we must wait for that, for the rest of their story. I have not yet imagined it as it should be imagined. I have not yet found the words, the correct words to speak that part of the story. Perhaps next time. I am tired now. All this makes me so tired.

To Whom It May Concern

Still waiting at the airport, the cousin is reading a letter, an old letter Sarah wrote fifteen years ago. He took that letter with him before leaving, as if to prove to himself that all this time he had been thinking about her.

During the early years the cousins exchanged letters regularly, but with time these became more distant, less detailed, and finally they stopped altogether. It seemed that they had nothing more to say to each other, or whatever there was to say seemed uninteresting. Unimportant. Twenty years passed before he wrote to Sarah again.

Raymond Federman

He was back in the country where he and Sarah were born. Some of his work was even being shown there. In fact, he found it ironic that the exhibition was held at the museum built on the spot where Aunt Basha's building once stood. Sarah smiled when she read that in his letter. He told her how he went to see the house where she used to live, and how he stood a long time in front of the building remembering the day, at the end of the war, when he saw her standing alone in the street.

During that visit he went to all the places he had known in his childhood. He looked at them without emotion. He felt cut off from all this. Even when he went inside the closet where his mother had hidden him, he felt nothing. A family was now living in the small apartment, and the closet was full of their things. But being here, where it all started, he suddenly had a need to re-establish contact with Sarah. Sitting in a café, he wrote to her. He tried to give his letter a casual and detached tone, as if all that had happened meant little to him now. But he did say, how he thought about her all the time, even if he had not written in so many years.

Sarah's response moved him deeply.

To Whom It May Concern

What a great surprise to read you again after so many years. Me too, I often think of you, and remember how we were, and what happened to us. I must admit that I was very moved by your letter. It would have been such a joy for me to be with you when you went back to all the places we knew. It is a beautiful city, in spite of all. I imagine you are reliving all this with apprehension and emotion.

Thank you for sending me the article about you, I had no idea you had become such an important artist. I'm so happy for you, so proud of you. I thank you also for the photographs. You look just the same. The gray at the temples makes you look so distinguished. I think I would recognize you anywhere. I like the picture of your daughter too. She's beautiful. She has your mother's eyes. But no picture of your wife. Next time remember to send one. You don't say much about your work. What kind of sculptures do you make? I would like so much to see them.

As for me, what can I say? Nothing has changed. Elie and I work hard all the time. I will say as you did, that we are relatively content with our lives, but sometimes I think we have wasted our best years with work. Of course, we could say we have built a country. Oh, what a big heavy phrase! We are a minority here surrounded everywhere by hostility, and every incident of violence affects us deeply.

You ask that I tell you everything we do, but it's hard to know what will interest you. My children are very important to me. We are very close. I wish you could meet Yossi and Tamar. They are growing, and Elie and I are very concerned about their education. As for me? What can I say? That with age my face is starting to show some wrinkles. Perhaps I am finally becoming more mature. To avoid feeling cut off I try to keep informed about what goes on in the world, but it's not easy. There isn't much time left work. I read. Listen to music. Classical music. That's what I listen to the most.

Elie, whom I hope you will meet someday, is so good to me. Marrying him was certainly the most successful thing I did in my entire life. Tell me about your wife. How you met, what she does. Maybe soon the two of you can come visit here. It's a beautiful place, you'll see. I would like so much to see you, meet your wife, look at your daughter. Embrace all of you. Write soon again, write and give lots of details.

Over the years, he often read and reread this letter, but he did not write again, for fifteen years. Not until he received the invitation from the museum. Sarah did not write either. Perhaps they stopped for fear of the banality of what is said in letters. They both often thought of writing, but they didn't. And yet before leaving, he remembered that letter. Searched for it. Reread it. Put it in his pocket to read again on the plane.

The cousin folds the letter and puts it away. He tries to imagine the scene at the airport when he arrives and sees Sarah waving at him with tears in her eyes. Excesses of emotion always embarrass him. To avoid that moment, he retreats into the past and finds himself once again with Sarah in that cellar where the two of them lived after the war. He hears her distant voice as she tries to tell him what had happened.

So you too were on a farm, he remembers saying to her ...

It was not really a farm, Sarah explained, it was just a house in the country. The old woman who kept me had chickens and ducks and some rabbits. And there was also a pig. A huge pig. At first I was scared of that pig. I had to feed him. I had never been that close to a pig. But after a while I began to like him. I called him Marius. The cousin remembers the smile on Sarah's face when she said that. But one day two men came from a nearby farm and they took the pig inside a barn and killed him. I didn't see how they did it, I only heard the squeals. It was horrible. But after that we had lots of meat for weeks. Josette sometimes came to visit, on Sundays. I don't think the old woman was her grandmother, though she always called her Grandmama. On Sundays, the three of us went to church. Josette and the grandmother taught me how to pray. Then Josette didn't come any more. I asked the grandmother where she was, but she didn't know. One morning I got up late because the old woman had not come to wake me as she always did. I hurried to get dressed. I thought she would be angry because I had not fed the animals yet. When I came into the kitchen, she was not there, and the fireplace had not been lit. It was cold that day. I looked outside for the old woman. The chickens and the ducks were still in their coop making a lot of noise. She was not there. I went back inside the house and knocked on the door of her bedroom. There was no answer. So I opened the door, and I saw the grandmother still asleep in bed. I walked over and touched her to wake her, but she didn't wake up. Her body was cold. She was dead.

She had been very kind to me. Except that she made me do all the work around the house. Sometimes when she kissed me I could feel the hair on her face. She had a little mustache like a man, and it scratched when she kissed me. Also, sometimes when it was very cold, she made me sleep with her in her bed, and she would put her arms around me and hold me tight. When I found her dead I didn't know what to do. Her house was far from other houses. I stood a long time next to the bed looking at her. Her face was all white, and her eyes half-open, and I could see she had no teeth in her mouth, but it wasn't scary. Then I remembered that the animals had not been fed. I went out into the yard, gave some grains to the chickens and the ducks, and some carrots to the rabbits. The pig was not there any more. He had already been killed. I saw the mailman coming toward the house on his bicycle and I rushed to him and told him about the grandmother. He said not to touch anything, and that I should not go in the bedroom, and he would be right back. He climbed on his bicycle and pedaled away hard. Soon he returned with other people. I recognized some of them from the church. Then the priest came and they all sat around the table in the kitchen and talked very softly. I sat by myself in a corner of the room. I think they were talking about me. When they finally got up, the priest told me that I would stay with him in his house now. He told me to gather my things. I made a little bundle with my clothes, and I rode to his house sitting on the back of his bicycle. I don't know what they did with the old woman.

At first I liked it better at the house of the priest because I didn't have to do much work. There was a woman who came during the day to

Raymond Federman

cook for the priest and clean his house. She was nice to me. It was a very small house. Just one large room connected to the church by another small narrow room, like a corridor. The priest, everybody called him Father, used the large room where he had his bed and a huge table where he did his writing. I slept in the small room, underneath the staircase that led to the attic. At night I could hear the rats moving above me. I was scared and cold all the time. The people who came to the church were saying that it was one of the worst winters they had ever seen. One night, it was snowing hard that night, the priest said that if I was too cold I could come and sleep in his bed with him. So I went and got under the thick blankets of his bed. I was trembling ...

Sarah would always stop there, and leave her cousin stranded in the middle of her story, and he never learned the rest. He would wait for her to continue, but she would remain silent, or she would say, I often thought of my mother and father and my brothers when I lived with the priest. I often prayed for them the way Josette and the grandmother had taught me ... I stayed in that house with the priest until the end of the war ... I was very unhappy ... and then I came back to the city and I found you ...

152

To Whom It May Concern

The cousin gets up and walks around the waiting lounge. He suddenly feels anxious -- anxious for his plane to depart so he can see Sarah again.

To Whom It May Concern

Remember how I indicated some time ago that this story should begin with a delay. I now realize that all I have said so far has been that delay. An uncalculated postponement. And yet it is that very postponement which makes me believe that perhaps I am already deep into the story, fragmented and undelineated as it may be. What was delayed was not the process nor the beginning, but the unforeseeable end. The beginning is now in place. It happened inadvertently.

Having come this far, since last November, the problem I confront now is no longer that of finding a beginning for this story, but of bringing it to a compelling end. The problem is no longer how to launch the story

Raymond Federman

of the two cousins, but of discovering if they will be capable of tenderness and understanding when they meet again and embrace!

This will not happen by rushing to an easy resolution, but by returning to where it all started. Back to the soldiers and the round-up on that July day. Back to the loaf of bread left behind with the woman next door. Back to the trucks on the square, the little girl with the yoyo, and Aunt Basha rushing to her cowardly survival. Back to Sarah wandering in the city, and to Josette who by wiping away Sarah's tears became enmeshed in history. And back also to the closet where the cousin defecated his fear, and up to the roof where he left his parcel of excrement.

All these months I've been facing toward an unthinkable end, while looking over my shoulder at an impossible beginning. Now I must turn to face the beginning, and as I look over my shoulder I will perhaps see the end. For ultimately the story of Sarah and her cousin will not be resolved in their final embrace, but in the difficulty that led to that embrace.

I know that one should never look back toward the noise from which one came. Lot's wife became a pillar of salt when she turned toward

To Whom It May Concern

that noise. Sarah and her cousin, in the great gap that separates them, often turn toward the original chaos of their lives. That is their great weakness. And yet, it is the constant movement they make toward this chaos that gives them the strength to go on. I am tempted to believe that the cousin became a sculptor, a maker of statues, to avoid becoming a statue himself, and that Sarah erased, and keeps on erasing the family lines between her son and her dead brothers, between her son and her cousin just not to fall into the gap of their absence. For Sarah and her cousin the original chaos of their lives was the site of an absence. The carving, the molding, the scratching away, the erasing are attempts to bring back that which was absented. But these are futile and contradictory gestures because Sarah and her cousin have been condemned to live facing backward to stare into the great abyss of absence.

This does not give me much chance of being able to extort their story from them and bring it to an end, and yet this morning certain questions that come to my mind offer a bit of hope. For instance, what happened to the father's coat the boy wore when he stepped out of the closet? And what happened to the things the boy found in the coat pockets? Perhaps it is this concern for the trivial details of the cousins' adventure that will validate their story. Yes, what happened to the loaf of bread Sarah left with the neighbor? What happened to the yoyo the little girl on the square showed Sarah before being trucked away? And what happened to the package the boy left on the roof? For me the drama of this story is the simplicity of these questions.

The coat was lost. Abandoned somewhere. Or it became so worn that eventually it disintegrated into the wind, like the boy's package of excrement on the roof. Unless birds came to peck at that package, and moths and rats devoured what was left of the coat. But the objects the boy found in the coat pockets, the coin, the key, and even the pencil stub, all these he kept. Not the safety pin though. He lost it, or perhaps used it one day when in need. A safety pin is always useful, especially during a small crisis. Maybe he used the safety pin to repair a hole in the seat of his pants. But the coin, the key, and the pencil stub, these he kept all these years. He kept them in a shoe box, with Sarah's letters and photographs. Preparing for this trip, he reread Sarah's letters and looked at her pictures, and there, at the bottom of the box, he found the coin, the key, and the pencil stub. He held them in his hand for a moment, and then he began doodling with the pencil, wondering if some of his father's paintings had been sketched with it. All these years he treasured these little things left behind by his father. He often wished he could have found some of his paintings. But none remained. Of his mother and sisters, he reflected as he closed the shoe box, he had nothing. No signs of their passage in this world. Not even a snapshot. Over the years their faces had become blurred images. He could not remember a single sentence that passed between them. He wondered if Sarah had saved anything of her parents and brothers. As he put the coin, the key, and the pencil stub in his pocket to show Sarah, he thought how she would probably smile at the sight of these measly remains.

In the shoe box he also found the yellow patch that was sewn on his father's coat and which he tore off when he stepped out the closet and saw in the moonlight that it was there on his chest. But unlike Sarah who threw away her patch, he kept this one. He kept it not to remind himself of the shame and humiliation it had brought, but because it belonged to his father.

As for the loaf of bread. The woman and her husband ate it for dinner that night. It was still fresh. And the yoyo? It got lost in the great commotion.

Eventually the neighbor forgot about Sarah and her family. She went on with her life. It was hard during the war, especially toward the end when there was hardly any food, and every night planes would come to drop bombs on the city. But one day the war ended and life returned to normal. Except that many people who had been taken away never returned. Sometimes the woman and her husband, while sitting at the table, would talk about the war and remember how difficult it had been, and even wonder what ever happened to all the people who disappeared. She never mentioned to her husband that for a moment she held in her hand the destiny of the little girl who used to live next door.

One day, soon after her cousin went away and left her with Marco and Olga, Sarah went with the baby carriage to her old neighborhood, and she saw the woman coming toward her in the street. She recognized her immediately. She had not changed. Sarah wanted to turn and run, but the woman had seen her, even though she seemed unsure at first who this young girl with the baby carriage was. As she moved toward Sarah she stared intently as if trying to recognize someone she knew. When she got closer, she suddenly shouted, oh it's you! It's you! You're back!

Sarah said nothing. She couldn't. She felt something hard rising in her throat. She didn't know if she was supposed to become angry and shout vile things at this woman, or just shrug her shoulders and tell her calmly that everything was fine.

To Whom It May Concern

What happened? How was it? The woman asked as if truly concerned. She was next to Sarah now and she leaned over the carriage to look at the baby. Oh what a lovely little baby, she said, what a pretty face. Is it yours?

Sarah shook her head ...

Of course not, you're still much too young to have a baby, the woman said with a forced smile.

Sarah wanted to run, to push this woman out of her way and run, but the woman held her by the arm and said, I'm so glad you're back, oh you don't know how glad I am.

Again Sarah did not speak. She just jerked her arm out of the woman's grip and started walking. The woman caught up with her and said, you must come for dinner one night. Promise you will. We're still in the same apartment. Then you can tell us everything. You will come, won't you? I'll fix something nice.

Of course Sarah never went. But had she gone, she would probably have seen things that once belonged to her mother. Old dishes and silverware now mixed with the woman's own, a faded table cloth still bearing her mother's embroidered initials. Perhaps she would have recognized some of the furniture. Nothing much. Just little things the people in the building took from the apartment once they knew Sarah's family was not coming back. And why not? Why should these things have gone to waste?

After Sarah left for the desert, she soon forgot this woman. She became irrelevant. But once in a while Sarah would remember Josette and wonder what happened to her. After the war she tried to find her. She and her cousin even went to the street where Josette used to stand in doorways and asked some of the girls there if they knew Josette and where she was. None of them seemed to remember a girl by that name. She had reddish hair and freckles, and she always wore purple clothes, Sarah explained.

One could speculate as to what happened to Josette, but that would only lead into more pathos. But wherever she is now, Josette too must sometimes remember fondly the little girl in tears who walked into her life to teach her compassion. That is why it is essential for Sarah and her cousin to listen again and again to the noise of their confused beginning. For they cannot escape the fatality of that beginning, they can only grow accustomed to it.

And so, just as the cousins keep returning to the original chaos of their lives to find justifications for their survival, it is there perhaps that I too will find the means of bringing their story to its conclusion. In the beginning ...

To Whom It May Concern

Wednesday, March 8

I'm stuck again. I spent the last four days wondering what to call this story. That's all I did. All I could do. It kept me awake four nights in a row, tossing and turning titles in my head. I am stalled, unable to move until I find the proper one.

It is true that along the way, these past months, I managed to propose a number of possible titles. A couple even won your approval. But you will recall that they were all dismissed or abandoned, one after the other.

Raymond Federman

First, it was simply SARAH. That didn't seem to be enough, for in leaving out the cousin, it didn't show the symmetry of the story. So it got expanded to SARAH & HER COUSIN. But that said too much, and no longer carried a promise of mystery.

For a while I toyed with the idea of THE MAKING & UNMAKING OF A BOOK. What self-indulgence, you said. Why point to the obvious. That one got quickly dropped.

After that I seriously considered THE CHRONICLE OF A DIS-ASTER. It seemed appropriate enough for what was happening or not happening at the time. Again you were dissatisfied, saying that if DISASTER referred to the unforgivable enormity it reduced it to banality, and if it referred to the telling of the story itself, it reduced it to triviality. You had a point there.

For a couple of weeks I felt delighted with A SEASON OF COMFORT. But you argued that it should really be A SEASON OF DISCOM-FORT. I disagreed, pointing out that DISCOMFORT would kill the irony of the title. Eventually both were dismissed. They were too lyrical anyway for our purpose. And misleading, because finally it is not the writer's winter of despair that should be emphasized here, but the spring of anxiety that confronts the two cousins.

So here I am. Without a title again, unable to proceed in any direction. I could go back to the unpromising SARAH, or even SARAH & HER COUSIN, and leave it at that, but that would be a form of regression. And so this morning, as I continue searching for the right combination of words on which to hang this story, I suddenly remember how you once questioned the vagueness I decided to impose on the cousins' lives, vagueness of time and place, and it occurs to me that perhaps their story should be called HERE & ELSEWHERE. The HERE being the place where you and I have been united with words, and the ELSEWHERE the site where Sarah and her cousin have been separated by events. HERE where the story is trying to be told, ELSEWHERE where it happened.

There is also the temptation of FURTHER ABANDONMENT since the story, and what nourishes it are constantly being abandoned. But finally, having to face the fact that the whole thing may never reach coherence and forever remain the epistolary fragments you have before you, why not simply say that it is addressed, in its indecision and formlessness, TO WHOM IT MAY CONCERN, and get on with it.

Raymond Federman

Have we not always delighted ourselves and others with vagueness and misdirection? If this book is ever to be accepted, it will only be by those who are concerned with what is told here, or cannot be told.

Vagueness and misdirection. I have seriously considered dropping all the names here. The names of people, as I have done for places. Even Sarah's. Make everybody anonymous. Nameless. Refer to them only as cousins, children, neighbors, soldiers, enemies, friends. After all this is a story of erasures. Then why not erase all traces of pretense, and have a story that empties itself of references.

Something is going on this morning. Definitely. Even if I can't figure it out. In the midst of all this groping it occurs to me that I may be the exclusive interpreter of the dark side of this story. It's uncanny to feel this way. It makes one almost believe in fate. How exquisitely absurd. But perhaps it is in this attempted appropriation that the necessity and singularity of the cousins' story will be found.

After I told how Sarah was abandoned and then hidden in a prostitute's room, and how her cousin was locked in a closet defecating his fear on a newspaper, I realized that finally theirs was not a very singular story. Many boys and girls were abandoned in the streets or left hidden in closets during the great war, and many kind-hearted people, prostitutes or nuns, took cognizance of these children and saved them, so that finally all this becomes banal.

How to deal then with the arrogance of what I have told so far of Sarah and her cousin? Perhaps that's what their story should be called: THE ARROGANCE OF STORY-TELLING.

To Whom It May Concern

Something always happens when alone in the dark one awaits the flashes that come with insomnia. There you are lying in bed, and bit by bit, as if someone were turning a key in the back of your head, that big butterfly key that makes mechanical toys move, your nerves extend. They stretch, all along your arms, along your neck and down your spine. Your nerves get longer and more taut. Your eyes stretch too, so that the lids don't fit any more and you begin to stare. The staring is the main thing. You think you can see no matter how dark. And you can, but everything is flat and taut, with no thickness. And you think it will always be that way. Everything will remain flat. On the wall something jumps up and down. A tiny black spot, like a spider. A flat spider. That minute speck is the sleep you are trying to catch. So you concentrate on it, try to make it bigger so you can crawl inside and sleep. You try hard to convince yourself it is growing and sleep is coming so you won't have to think any more, think of the book you're supposed to be writing that is not being written. And you stare. You stare so hard your eyeballs hurt, but you cannot hold the dark spot in place. It keeps moving. Up and down. It shrinks. Disappears. Comes back. Then suddenly the spider slides off to one side, up the wall, onto the ceiling. You can't pin it down. So you chase it, watch for it to hold still so you can make it grow again. And then comes the pain of surrender when the craving for sleep becomes a torture. It's maddening ...

It happened again last night. I was chasing that spider all over the walls and ceiling of the bedroom. The wife asleep next to me, or pretending to be. Maybe she was chasing her own spider. I was beginning to enjoy the chase, in spite of the anguish, when suddenly the spider became a bright spot of light, a yellow star on the wall, and it grew and grew until it exploded into a luminous screen, a movie screen, and the specks of sleeplessness turned into images. Right there before me. And I stared in amazement.

On the screen I saw Sarah and her cousin, and they were so real. Exactly the way I always imagined them. They were sitting in a garden.

To Whom It May Concern

The garden in the back of Sarah's house, on the edge of the desert. I could see the sand stretching to the horizon where the blue gray line of day was fading. It was evening. The cousins were sitting in deep lawn chairs facing each other, surrounded by twilight. Somehow while chasing that spider I had managed to project forward. The cousin was no longer waiting at the airport. His plane had arrived at the place of reunion. And now he was with Sarah, the first evening of his visit, in the garden behind her house, and they were talking. Asking each other the questions that had not been asked for thirty-five years.

But perhaps it was not me who leaped ahead into time, but the cousin, and I simply followed him, as I had my black spider on the wall. While waiting at the airport, apprehensive about seeing Sarah, eyes closed, or else staring into the non-space of the waiting hall, the cousin was rehearsing what he would say when Sarah would ask about his life and his work, and even rehearsing what she would say about herself. The scene I was watching was not on the wall of my bedroom, nor inside my head. It was unfolding, being played in the cousin's mind, and somehow I had managed to lodge myself there. I was no longer the director of the cousins' drama, just one of its spectators.

Raymond Federman

The cousins were talking softly. I had to strain to hear what they were saying. Strain also to make out their faces in the cool darkness slowly settling over the desert. Sarah was asking her cousin about his work, and he was explaining, as he had never done before, not even to himself, that what he made were not really sculptures, but objects without form made of raw emotions. He was speaking slowly but passionately. Not lecturing, as he had tendency to do whenever he discussed his work, but as if the way Sarah had phrased her question called for a simple and deliberate answer. It was important to him that she understood what he was saying.

The cousin had expected to feel awkward with Sarah, even shy and distant after all these years. But he wasn't, and neither was Sarah. She had anticipated that when her cousin would appear at the airport she would move toward him with doubt and panic. Instead she immediately felt at ease when he held her in his arms, and the long years of separation were erased.

Later, sitting at the dinner table together with Elie, they were surprised at how simply and easily the words flowed between them. Then Elie excused himself and went to bed when the cousins stepped out into the garden. Puffing on a cigarette, the cousin was now explaining his work.

To Whom It May Concern

Later it would be Sarah's turn to tell about her life and her work in the desert.

You see, he was saying, one cannot give shape to sentiments, one cannot mold emotions into neat forms. They simply flow in the world. The human body does not end with lines. That is why the presence of man in space is dramatic. The great paradox of that hard substance sculptors make is that it delimits immobility and organizes space into silence. Sculptures are lifeless things. And yet, for a long time I tried to give form to sentiments, tried to shape emotions into objects, but I failed. I only produced geometry. There was nothing profound or meaningful in that work. It is only when sculpture defies geometry that it becomes compassionate and dramatic, but then it ceases to be sculpture. And so one day I abandoned the security of form and the delight of symmetry and rendered my work shapeless, but that too led to failure.

How can you say that, Sarah interrupted, how can you say you failed when your work is recognized all over the world, even in a small insignificant country like this one.

That means nothing. That kind of recognition comes easily, and goes easily. I failed because I have not been able to give shape to what can never be recovered. The cousin paused turning his head toward the desert. Sarah did not ask what could not be recovered, but as if her silence were a question he offered the answer: absence that's what can never be recovered, absence. And again there was silence between them. And I was there with them in that silence. Then, as if finishing a sentence that had begun in his head, he said, you must understand, I am caught between the desire for fame and the need for oblivion. And so I am vain enough to search in every book for the mention of my name, but sardonic enough to mock my own eagerness. Perhaps this struggle against my own art will remain my most important and most durable achievement. Of course, I will never know, he added, shrugging his shoulders and raising his hands in an equivocal gesture.

Though what her cousin was saying was vague and abstract, Sarah understood what he meant. She had not yet seen his sculptures at the museum, the exhibition was to open officially the following day, and she would be there with him, but already she knew that his work would be obscure and savage, and yet she knew she would like it even if she did not understand. Yes, she knew in advance that his sculptures would be strange and perhaps disturbing, but she also knew that they would be profound by their very refusal of profundity, and Sarah said that to her cousin.

An affectionate smile came on his face. He raised one hand as if to reach for Sarah, but it remained suspended in mid-air pointing to something in the dark. You haven't changed at all, he said. Still as kind and thoughtful as the day I left you at the train station. How young, how young and innocent we were. No. No we were already old and ... he paused, his mouth half-open as if waiting for a word to take shape ... old and used, he finally said, and again he waited for the words ... You don't know how often I thought of you standing there on the train platform. You were trying so hard not to cry as you waved goodbye. You cannot imagine how terrible I felt for having left you behind.

He was surprised at himself to have been able to say that.

It was getting darker, though a glow from the horizon still lingered over the desert. Sarah's face was also glowing. After having had the courage to hide her longing for so many years, she now lacked the strength to hide her happiness.

The cousins continued to talk, and I listened, hoping that they would not stop and fearing that they would. Sarah was telling how she and Elie had built this house with stones and sand from the desert, and how they had raised their children in this house. Yossi and Tamar are so excited about meeting you. They will be at the museum tomorrow. Perhaps you will recognize something of your father or of my mother in their eyes. They have given us a lot of joy. A lot of worries too. This is not an easy place to raise children. Elie is a quiet man, as you saw, quiet and gentle, but he can become formidable and fearless when it comes to protect those he loves. We have worked hard together, and except for our children there is not much to show for it. In this country everything is in a constant state of transition and erosion. The past does not belong to anyone, and nor will the future. When we first came here this place looked like a dead volcano. It was an empty place. We tried to make it full, but the desert is stubborn, it refuses progress. The desert does not give, it takes. One becomes a lizard here, one starts resembling the desert sand.

While listening to Sarah the cousin was admiring her quiet strength, her calm and lucidity, but especially he admired her beauty. He had expected Sarah to be sentimental and self- pitying, instead he found only strength in her. The frail and frightened young girl he left behind at the train station had become a beautiful woman. Even though her face was parched by the desert sun, her hands dry and wrinkled, her body bent and overly muscular, there was beauty in her gestures, in the way she held her head slightly tilted to one side, in the way she looked into the distance as if expecting someone to appear there suddenly. There was beauty too in the way she spoke. She made everything sound so simple, so uncomplicated.

Sarah was now describing how she had extorted her garden from the desert. She loved this garden with its flowers, its bit of grass and stubborn plants. In the evening, after the long hours in the fields of the camp farm, she spent time in her garden until it was too dark to see. She pulled weeds from the flower beds, watered the plants, cut the dry leaves, or just sat meditating while her fingers played with a leaf or the petal of a flower. Elie rarely went into the garden. He stayed in the house when Sarah was out there. He read, put some order in his albums of photographs, listened to music. He understood the need Sarah had to be alone.

In the evening in her garden Sarah meditated about life. What she experienced as a child during the war, and later as a young woman when she came here, taught her the supreme value not of art but of life. Here in the desert Sarah learned to eliminate all emotional luxuries. The time she spent in her garden meditating while her hands were busy with flowers was an essential part of the day. After so many years in this land of promises, many left unfulfilled, she learned that one must be calm inside to capture the outside.

This Sarah was trying to explain to her cousin for she sensed that there was great turmoil inside of him even though he appeared composed and self-assured. But how could she make him understand the importance of calmness, or even the necessity of failure?

Here flowers grow all year long if one takes care of them, Sarah explained to her cousin who had reached for a tulip next to his chair, not to pluck it, but to touch its soft petals. These flowers are not a luxury, she said, they are a necessity. Here what is not a necessity is an encumbrance.

The cousin did not say anything, he just shook his head in a slow gesture of approbation ...

A voice on the loudspeaker in the waiting hall of the airport announces the departure of a plane, but the announcement is not about his plane.

To Whom It May Concern

Eyes still closed, head shaking slightly, he continues to listen to Sarah speak in the distance.

The cousin had never seen Sarah's house, none of the photographs she sent showed the house, and yet as he projects ahead into time he is able to imagine it just as it is. A simple house, crude even in its structure, but solid and comfortable. Just right. The garden too. He can see the garden where he will sit with Sarah to talk.

And me too, last night, as I stared at the walls of my bedroom, I could see the house and the garden, and the cousins sitting in the dusk, and I heard Sarah ask her cousin if he was happy.

Happy! What does that mean? The cousin was up now. He had taken a few steps toward the edge of the garden. His back to Sarah. He was reflecting on how the flowers and the plants seemed to defy the barren sand next to them.

Since he arrived late in the day, the cousin had not yet seen the fields which the people of the camp farm had wrested from the desert. The next day, when Sarah and Elie will show him the fields, he will realize that while he wrestled alone with his pieces of metal and stone, they had wrestled with the desert to carve out these fields, and he will understand that theirs was the greater struggle, and the greater success, even though Sarah will insist that they have failed.

Happy! He repeated turning toward Sarah. Can one ever be happy? Sure, my wife and my daughter have given me happiness, but as soon as one admits to happiness one also loses it, and it becomes futile to move toward happiness in order to lose it again. He didn't mean to sound so ponderous. So negative. With Sarah he wanted to use clear and positive words. But suddenly he felt ill-at-ease, tense, clumsy in his own words, and the more he tried to explain himself the more he seemed to reopen the gap between them, the distance that had closed so instantly when they embraced at the airport.

Sarah, on the contrary, felt more and more comfortable as she watched her cousin gesticulate before her as he spoke. He was exactly the way she had expected him to be. Complex and abstract, but also shy and sensitive, and easily decipherable. Earlier, while waiting for him to arrive, she thought she would be intimidated by him, but instead she immediately felt at ease and in control. Not at all the timid insecure little sister she was to him years ago, but like an older sister who looks

182

upon a younger brother with ironic tenderness. And so Sarah showed no hesitation in asking endless questions about his life, about his wife and daughter. Questions which he seemed unable to ask of Sarah, perhaps because being here and seeing how she lived was sufficient for him. Sarah wanted to know everything, and so, almost in spite of himself, he revealed more than he was accustomed to, and told Sarah how for years he struggled to find himself, and how one day he discovered his vocation and became obsessed with his art, how he met his wife and fell in love, and how together for twenty-five years they had maintained a dialogue which united them night and day, and he told Sarah how much he loved his wife and daughter, how important they were to him. How they understood him, accepted his moods, mocked his vanity and eagerness. Even his work, he told Sarah, was irrelevant compared to what they meant to him. He was surprised to have said this, but somehow with Sarah he felt he could say anything, say everything he had been unable to say all these years.

And yet it was not to talk about himself, about his family life, or even about his work that he had come here. He had come to learn, once and for all, what happened to Sarah during the war. He came to gain access to the dark events of Sarah's past, which would perhaps allow him to gain access to his own past. Of course, he knew that the access to an event of the past is never unmediated, that it is always manipulated by

Raymond Federman

false restitutions. But he also knew that one must resist such restitutions, even if it makes it impossible to reach the truth. Being here with Sarah he now understood that it was not through remembrances, however redeeming, that he and Sarah would resolve their incapacity to be happy, and this because of the arbitrary process at work in them which constantly displaces the original chaos of their lives toward its erasure.

Last night, as I listened to the cousins talk in that garden, as I watched them drifting from the initial happiness of their reunion into declarations of their failures, I realized that ultimately it will not be their story that will authenticate my work, but their faces which will testify to the centrality of what has to be recorded. Their faces and their presence.

And suddenly I heard Sarah say as if surfacing from a dark thought, what happened to us years ago remains a great wound for me.

After a moment of silence her cousin said, yes but it is out of that wound that you and I have shaped our lives. And then he added, the world in which we live at best offers a truncated and fallacious existence, it requires that either we close our eyes and forget or compromise. Sarah

184

did not reply, but she sensed that what he had just said was exactly what she too was thinking. How strange and yet logical the understanding that existed between them. It was as though they had never been separated, as though their thoughts had always converged.

As they sat in the garden, now in total darkness, suddenly their dialogue rendered my words meaningless. Listening to her cousin speak of his work, of his life as a sculptor, Sarah understood that it was no longer necessary to ask what she had been waiting thirty-five years to ask. To ask him to tell her what happened after he left the closet. The way he talked about his work and his life was the answer. And the cousin too understood that he no longer needed to ask what happened after the old woman died and the priest took her in. Sarah's garden, and what she said of the flowers and the desert was enough. Yes, the flowers and the desert were the answers to the questions he had been waiting to ask for so many years.

It had taken thirty-five years of absence from each other for the cousins to learn that strength does not come with knowledge, nor with remembrance, nor with recognition, but with small gestures and insignificant words. And so, as I continued to listen to the cousins, their faces fading into darkness, their voices becoming more and more faint,

Raymond Federman

I realized that their story would always remain unfinished ... and yet, even though sleep was finally coming to me, I pushed it away so that I could continue to listen to them ...